SONAM'S SURPRISE

Nikki Nichols
Illustrated by Niroj Bade

Sharpgiving Press
Seattle

Cover by Claudie C. Bergeron
Illustrations by Niroj Bade
Photo of the author by John Switten

ISBN: 979-8-9933477-9-0

https://sharpgiving.com/Nichols/SonamsSurprise

Go to our website to see
videos and photos, taken in Nepal,
that bring the story to life.
You'll also find other treasures there.

For Sherpa Children
and
All Nepali Children

One

Chreeeee, *chreeeee*, the geese called as they flew overhead.

I looked up into the bright blue sky, on that sunny October day, and saw Bar-Headed Geese flying in a V-formation.

It seemed they wanted my attention and were calling for me to follow them. Where would they lead me?

Then I heard another sound, "Eeeyeeey-eeeyeeee!"

What was that sound? It wasn't a bell, though sometimes I heard yaks' bells in the distance. It wasn't the sound of a lamb bleating, a sound I often heard since I tended so many sheep. It was weird to hear all those sounds. Hearing them and seeing the birds in formation made me think it was a day in which something extraordinary would happen.

However, Mother would say, "My son, you have a wild imagination. You daydream about adventures, extraordinary events, and exotic places. Dream all you want but the reality is you are just a shepherd."

Usually I did daydream; I drew pictures, or wrote my name, Sonam Sherpa, in the dirt to while away the hours as I tended our family's Tibetan sheep on the steep, rocky hillside in Nepal. Time moved as slowly as the clouds drifted overhead. But not that day!

I loved my sheep and wanted to protect them, but I couldn't imagine being a shepherd for the rest of my life. I was curious about a lot of things, and I wanted to learn a lot more. Some things I was curious about were: *What's it like inside a lamb's body? How can a bird fly over the top of the world's highest mountain? Why does it snow? How can a doctor heal a person's disease? Some climbers live far away from Nepal; what's life like where they live? What is it like inside the palace where the king of Nepal lives? Why do some people become artists and others become farmers?* There was so much to learn!

I was in the highest grade at the school in Khumjung, and I was one of the best students in the whole school. I wanted to go to an excellent secondary school, but to do that I would have to move away from my home village. Though Papa wanted me to become the educated son who would care for my mother and father in their old age, we didn't have enough money to feed the family and send me away to school.

I had an idea of my own for how I could earn some of the money to pay for school! I could sell some sheep, though my parents wouldn't like me to sell the ones we have now. They needed them for milk and wool. Instead, I would breed some of our sheep, raise the little ones, and sell them when they were mature. The one problem with that plan was that it would take at least five months, and I needed the money soon to register for school.

Then I had a better idea: *Perhaps I can get some of the money I need for school by helping Uncle Mingma on the house he's building. If he has me bring him things he needs, he can stay at the construction site.* I hoped he would be able to pay me enough and in time to register.

I remembered that Uncle also wanted to build a special house for the famous climber, Sir Edmund Hillary, but he didn't have much time because Sir Hillary was coming back to our village in about four months. *With me as his helper, Uncle can begin Sir Hillary's house sooner and work faster.* I would talk to Uncle Mingma that night about my idea.

Here was the best idea—it was a wild dream! What if someone offered to pay for my schooling? If that happened, I would quickly trade them the sickle and rope I used to herd the sheep. My teacher, Pemba, told me about a very special school in Kathmandu called the Budhanilkantha School.

"That school is better than the one in Khumjung" she explained, "and each year they send a representative to each region in the country, including Khumjung, to test students to see if any qualify for their school. A student who qualifies can get a scholarship."

Maybe that could be me! That would be a dream come true! I needed to find out when the next test date would be.

It seemed like a slim chance that I would be one of the few to get a scholarship, so I still hoped to work for Uncle Mingma. Otherwise, I'd have to tend sheep for the rest of my life. If I could get a lot more education, I, an insignificant peasant boy, could become a doctor, a famous artist, or . . . the sky's the limit to what I could become!

"Eeyeeyeeyeeyeeyee!"

That was the same sound I heard before. What could it be? An injured human? A wild animal?

"Eeyeeyeeyeee . . . Oooooooome ooooooooow!"

There it was again, but this time there was more, "Hey nephew! Nephew Sonam Sherpa, Come Hooooome NOOOOOOW!"

It was Uncle Mingma's voice, but he never called me in the middle of the day! *Something must be wrong.*

I ran down the steep hillside, as fast as a snow leopard, my twenty sheep right behind me. I burst through the doorway of my family's stone hut and climbed up the ladder as fast as I could!

4

Out of breath, I coughed as I entered the smoky room where my grandma cooks in a copper pot over an open fire, and where the family spends most of our time.

There I saw an unusual sight! *A stranger!* He was a tall, handsome young man, dressed in beautiful clothing: a blue V-neck sweater of fine wool, gray jacket, gray corduroy trousers, and a rectangular black, *topi* hat. He was engaged in conversation with Grandma and Uncle Mingma. Grandma served him roasted potatoes cooked under hot coals, on a dish along with some vegetable *tarkari*. My mouth watered at the nutty aroma of the roasted potatoes and the savory vegetables.

Grandma made some of her tasty Tibetan butter tea for me. She told me to sit with her and Uncle and the stranger.

Who was that man? I wondered. In a hushed tone, I asked, "Uncle, why did you call me?"

"Nephew," intoned Uncle Mingma, his voice respectful and serious. "This is *Hajur* Phura Tharkey, (Purr-a Tar-key) a very dignified messenger sent by the king to find *you!*"

We greeted each other with a slight bow and folded hands and said, "*Namaste.*"

Uncle continued, "He has a summons signed by the king and sealed in red ink with his official stamp. You must appear before the king in the palace in Kathmandu as soon as possible."

My eyes grew as big as saucers. "You are going to take *me* with you?" I asked with a bit of fear and much curiosity.

"Yes, and one of your family members will accompany us on this journey."

I shook my head in disbelief and whispered to Uncle, "Are you sure? Why me?"

I sat by Uncle and paid close attention to the conversation he and Grandma were having with Phura Tharkey. I tried to only listen, but I had to ask, "Why did the king send you to find me, an eleven-year-old, peasant boy? How does he even know I exist? Where does the king live? How did you get here?"

Phura Tharkey responded in a dignified way, "King Birendra sent me on a mission to walk to your village, Khumjung, to become familiar with the land, the people, and the culture. When I return to Kathmandu, I am to report to him all the things I learned. He would love to visit each village in the kingdom and become acquainted with the many different cultures of Nepal, but the king has many responsibilities. His calendar is so full that he commissioned me to be his emissary. For most of my life I have lived near the king while he taught me what he desires to know about our people and the country of Nepal. In order for me to be of even greater value to him, he sent me to the university to study Cultural Geography. There I studied many cultures and the many ways people interact with one another and the natural environment. The king instructed me to become familiar with the unique culture of your village, to meet you and your family, and to bring you, Sonam, back with me to meet him. The king has a problem that he needs you to help him solve. He did not give me any details about the problem. He told me that he needs Sonam Sherpa of Khumjung to come to Kathmandu, and there he will tell you in person what he wants you to do to help him solve this problem."

This surprised me. "Does the king have other children help him solve his problems?" I asked.

Phura Tharkey replied, "Yes, some children take care of animals in the palace courtyard: the elephants that amble around the grounds and the koi in the pond. Some climb the fruit trees on the palace grounds to pick the fruit to serve to the staff."

"But those kids could all be from Kathmandu," I said. "Why did the king tell you to come all the way out to Khumjung to summon me?"

Phura Tharkey responded, "I do not know. I do know that the king loves the mountains and would have loved to come here himself, but he leaves the palace only on official business. We will need to leave Khumjung within two days."

"How long will we be gone?" I asked.

"I don't exactly know—perhaps a week or two," Phura Tharkey responded.

Oh No! I thought. *Now I'll never get enough money in time to register for the village secondary school, and I'll miss the date that the Budhanilkantha School exam will be given in Khumjung!*

I was afraid that something horrible might happen to me on the journey, then I'd not get to go to school, and my sheep would be without a shepherd. On the other hand, something wonderful could happen! Papa had told me more than once, "Nothing risked, nothing gained." The reality was that I didn't have a choice. The king had summoned me, so I must go!

But the king doesn't even know me, I thought. *Does he know something about me? Does he know I am a shepherd? (How would that be of any value to the king?) Does the king know I like to draw? (How would that help the king?)*

Then it occurred to me, perhaps the king knew about the day my best friend Apa and I tried to help our community. I remember what we discussed:

I ran to my friend as soon as I heard the foreigner's plan. "Apa! Some foreigners want to build a hotel close to our village where the fantastic view of Sagarmatha is! And they plan to call it Hotel Everest View after the foreigners' name for our beloved Sagarmatha, the world's highest mountain!"

Apa understood the problem immediately, "Nobody in Khumjung wants a hotel there! What can we do about it? How can we help our community?"

"I have an idea. What if we pull the survey stakes out of the ground at the site of the hotel so they won't be able to build it? Then the people of Khumjung will be happy."

Apa considered it a moment then answered, "That should be easy since we're both strong boys. Let's go on the next market day that's foggy and misty. That way no one will see us."

A few days later, on a foggy morning while herding our sheep, Apa came to me and said, "Sonam, it's market day today. Let's go to that hotel site now. We can leave the sheep for a little while. Nothing will happen to them."

"Ok let's go." With all my heart, I hoped nothing would happen to the sheep.

We got to the site and found that the stakes were securely planted in the rocky ground! We had to work hard to remove them. I had an idea.

"Apa, you push the stakes and I'll pull them. Push harder! Kick them!" We sweated and panted. "Let's use rocks to dig holes around them to loosen them."

Then I heard something that made me jump. "*Ah-ooo! Ah-ooo!*"

I yelled to Apa, "That's a wolf!"

I looked up and saw that it was headed toward my sheep! We ran fast, and when we got to the sheep the wolf was on its hind legs ready to attack one of them.

"Lead the sheep away from the wolf!" I yelled to Apa, but hearing my voice the wolf turned and charged towards me! Its upper lip was pulled back, its sharp incisor teeth ready to bite me. I stood tall and put my arms out to make my small eleven-year-old body look as big as possible. I stared into the mean orange eyes of the snarling wolf. One slow step at a time, I backed up.

Then I stumbled over a rock! With its ears and fur erect, the wolf crouched backward ready to attack me. My heart beat fast, sweat poured down my face, and my muscles tensed. I reached down, picked up a rock, and threw it as hard as I could!

When the rock hit the wolf above its left eye, it growled and leapt toward me!

I jumped sideways, and it missed me. Without breaking eye contact with the wolf, I grabbed another rock and threw it hard. It hit the wolf's forehead. The strike created a gaping wound.

Finally, the defeated wolf whimpered, lowered its head, flattened its ears, and crept away. *Phew!* We were all safe, Apa, my sheep, and I.

I was stunned and exhausted and wanted to collapse. As I recovered, my breathing and heart rate began to slow down. Instead of being the demise of me, it had almost been the end of the wolf! What a relief! Papa would be proud of me. With two rocks I maimed the wolf and protected myself and my sheep! From now on, I'll always carry two rocks with me.

"I wish we didn't have to go back to the hotel site," I told Apa, "I'd rather stay with the sheep and rest on the hillside."

"We have to go! We can't give up in the middle!" Apa replied. So we went back to the hotel site and continued our work.

"Apa, you push, and I'll pull the stakes. Push harder. Kick them."

"Sonam, you look exhausted, we can't do this much longer."

Finally, we got all sixteen of them out. We held up the stakes and cheered, "Yeah, we did it!"

Apa asked anxiously, "What shall we do with them? We can't leave them here and we can't take them back to Khumjung with us!"

I thought quickly, "You told me there's a cave close by. We could stash the stakes there. Where is it?"

"I'll lead you to it."

We gathered the stakes together and dashed across the slope.

Inside the cave, it smelled. "Bats have pooped in here!" I exclaimed. "Bats have diseases! We've got to get out of here!"

We ran toward the mouth of the cave where we spotted a boulder.

Apa yelled, "Let's put the stakes behind this boulder. No one will look for them here."

We threw the stakes down then raced out of the cave and back toward our sheep. We herded our sheep back to the village and got there just as it turned dark.

We never told anyone about our experience, so I didn't think anyone knew, but now in the smoky kitchen with Phura Tharkey, I wondered: *Did the king find out somehow? Maybe the king wants to punish me. Is that why he summoned me?*

Two

The smoky kitchen and living area pulled me back from my wandering memories. Phura Tharkey was still talking about the king, and I was still puzzled why he would summon an eleven-year-old peasant shepherd boy.

Will papa go with me to meet the king? If not him, then who?

I wondered about the king: *Does he have a family? Does he sleep in a bed? What was he like when he was my age?*

I wondered about Kathmandu: *What does it look like? Does it look like Khumjung?*

Again, Phura Tharkey's voice pulled me back. "The king told me he wants me to become familiar with your village, Khumjung, meet your family and some of the people who live here, and if possible, to meet some of Khumjung's leaders. Could you help me do those things?"

"Of course. I would be honored to do all that you have requested and to show you around our village," I responded.

It was a crisp, sunny, afternoon, a perfect time to introduce Phura Tharkey to our village. I led Grandma, Uncle Mingma, and Phura Tharkey down the ladder from our living quarters, through the area where the animals sleep, past where their food is stored, and out through the big wooden door.

We walked around the corner of the house where we saw my seven-year-old brother, Pasang.

"What is that boy doing?" Phura Tharkey asked me.

"He's my brother. I'll ask him to explain."

I called out to Pasang, "Hey Brother, tell our guest why you stick your hands in gooey yak poop?"

Pasang's eyes twinkled. "I make cakes. Would you like to taste one?"

Phura Tharkey looked worried. "Does he expect us to eat them?"

"No, they are fuel for the fire that Grandma cooks on," I assured him.

"They make very good fuel," Grandma commented adding, "Pasang, tell Phura Tharkey why you throw that yak poop at our freshly whitewashed house."

"It's so the cakes will dry. They don't smell and they don't leave marks. See how cool it looks with my handprint on each one?" Pasang said, as he danced with his hands. Then he asked, "Where are you going? Can I come too?"

"After you wash your filthy hands," I teased, "Of course you can join us. We are showing our guest around the village."

Pasang looked at Phura Tharkey with reservation and asked, "Who are you?"

"My name is Phura Tharkey."

"Phura Tharkey is a messenger from the king of Nepal; he came to see *me*!" I held my chest high with pride.

"Oh sure!" teased Pasang.

"It's true. He is the king's messenger." Only after Phura Tharkey nodded his head in agreement did Pasang believe me.

When we walked a little farther, I saw my sister in the *partetu* surrounded by the stone wall. Pointing, I told Phura Tharkey, "That's my little sister, Lakpa. She's eight years old. She helps my older brother Dorje, who is a farmer, plant potatoes in the *partetu*."

As I looked at her, I remembered the day I'd tried to help her earn some extra money. Before we took her bag of potatoes to the market, I put some stones the same size as the potatoes into her bag, so they'd weigh more and she'd get paid more. *Oh no, did that bag go to the royal palace?* I'd thought no one knew about that, but now I wondered if somehow the king knew. *Does he want to punish me for that? Is that why the king summoned me?*

Lhakpa ran over to us, pointed at Phura Tharkey, and asked, "Who is this man?"

"He is a messenger from the king. He came all the way from Kathmandu to meet me and take me with him to meet the king!" I explained.

"I don't believe you!" she said, cocking her head and pushing her long black hair aside from her pretty face. Then she looked at Phura Tharkey with awe and inquired, "Is it true you are a messenger from the king?"

"Yes, I am."

Lhakpa bowed her head, put her hands together, and in a quiet voice said "Namaste."

In return, he gave her a warm greeting.

I told Phura Tharkey "I think Pasang and Lakpa are cute, so sometimes I like to draw pictures of them as they do their chores."

"What do you draw with?" Phura Tharkey asked.

I showed him the little sketchbook I had made and explained, "I draw with pencils or sometimes charcoal that's left over after Grandma cooks our food. I like to draw pictures of my parents too, but they aren't home as much as my sister and brother. My father, Dakshi, sometimes sleeps on the mountainside because he teaches novice mountain guides how to lead extreme climbs. My mother, Chamba, leaves every morning before the sun rises to take the yaks up the hillside where they graze. Before they leave, she milks them and their deep, rumbling, grunting noises wake me up. I don't like to leave my warm, soft, yak wool, blanket that mother made for me and crawl out of bed into the cold room, but it's all worth it when I get to taste the fresh, sweet, milk in my chai."

"It is good milk," Lakpa chimed in.

"While your mother tends the yaks, you care for the sheep, is that right?

"She is with the yaks most of the day. I go to school in the morning and tend the sheep in the afternoon."

"Sonam, tell me about your sheep. What do you like about being a shepherd?" Phura Tharkey inquired.

"I like my sheep. They are smart and each one has a unique personality, so I gave each one a funny name. I named them after Nepalese cartoon characters like Meena, Raju, and Mithu. Sheep are impressive. They can see behind themselves even if they don't turn their heads!"

Phura Tharkey looked surprised and asked, "How can they do that?"

"Their eyes are special—they have horizontal, slit-shaped pupils. Another thing about sheep is they eat a lot. They can graze for seven hours each day, so I have to move my flock from place to place. If they grazed all day in one area, that would be dangerous; when I asked Dorje why, he told me it could cause erosion and landslides. Since we move around, I get to explore new areas and I like that."

"One day I found a cave. It's way up there. I pointed high up on the hillside next to the area where there'd been a landslide, at the base of Khumbila, the mountain that rises above Khumjung. I wanted to go inside it, but I wanted my older brother Dorje to go with me."

Uncle added, "I went in that cave one time. There are some interesting things in it."

Lakpa and Pasang in unison said, "We want to go! When can we go?"

Uncle replied, "When you are older, I'll take you there."

"It would be fun to take you there, Phura Tharkey, but it would take too much time. Instead, I'll tell you about the time I explored it with my older brother."

A few days after I found the cave, Dorje and I climbed up the steep hillside and went inside the cave. It was cool and moist.

"It's dark in here," I said to Dorje. "Our torch doesn't give much light."

"Yes and also the ceiling is very low, so we can't see far ahead," he replied, "so we'll have to crawl along the cave floor."

We crept along for a while.

In one place it felt like the ceiling was higher, so I stood up. "Ow!"

"Are you alright?"

"I hit my head on a stalactite," I explained, rubbing the place where it hurt.

Dorje looked above my head to see what had hit me. "Hey, look at those smoky marks on the wall. What do you think they are?"

"I don't know. Maybe ancient people caught a deer and cooked it in here?" I speculated.

"Maybe they sacrificed goats as a religious ritual," Dorje added.

"I wonder what else is in here. Let's go deeper into the cave."

Crawling further, I saw some faint red lines on the cave wall. "Look Dorje, see those markings. Do you think those are cave paintings?"

"Maybe, but it's difficult to tell what the pictures are supposed to be."

"That's too bad. I wish I could see them."

"Me too. But we better go back now, we've been in here quite a while."

"We were in the cave for about an hour," I explained to Phura Tharkey. "When we came out, we blinked our eyes a bunch of times as we adjusted to the bright daylight. Ever since we visited that cave, I've been curious about cave paintings."

This reminded Phura Tharkey: "Once I heard someone talk about ancient Buddhist cave paintings that are in western Nepal. They are supposed to be in excellent condition."

"I would love to see some well-preserved, ancient cave paintings! Phura Tharkey, can you tell me anything more about them?"

"No, but when we are in Kathmandu, we can ask the king what he knows about them. He's knowledgeable about art history."

That made me wonder, *What kind of paint did the people use long ago?* "I think it'd be fun to try to create a cave painting. I could draw pictures of my sheep, or the birds I see that fly overhead, or of the little animals I find under rocks. Maybe we can find some animals under these rocks. Let's look."

Lakpa, Pasang and I turned over several rocks and found worm trails, some little black insects, and a patch of brown wooly fur from a marmot. Phura Tharkey looked a little squeamish, but Pasang and Lakpa squealed with delight each time a new creature appeared.

"Birds like these rocks too," I explained. "The Himalayan Monal pheasant, our multi-colored national bird, searches on the ground around these rocks for insects to eat. It is a beautiful bird, and I feel lucky when I get to see one. Another favorite bird of mine is the long- tailed red-bellied Rosy Minivet, but they live in the forest."

Uncle added, "There are lots of different kinds of birds that live around Khumjung."

"Besides getting to see the birds and the little creatures under the rocks, these rocks are great places to play. Do you want to hear a story about one time when my friend, Apa, and I played Hide and Seek in the crevices of these big rocks?"

Phura Tharkey smiled, "Yes, that would be enjoyable."

I told Apa, "Shut your eyes and count to ten, then come look for me!"

I ran a little way down the hill then jumped into a gully. From my hiding place, I watched my friend leap over rocks and look down the steep cliff.

"Ha, ha, ha," my laughter echoed off the rocks.

Hearing my laugh, Apa soon found me. "What made you laugh?"

"You looked so funny when you jumped over rocks. You looked like a musk deer that leaps over rocks and darts amongst small bushes."

My words made Apa laugh too. "Now it's your turn, Sonam! You count to ten and I'll hide!"

"One, two, three, four, five, six, seven, eight, nine, ten. Here I come, ready or not!"

The sheep seemed to want to help me look, and we frolicked in the sunshine until they ran in all different directions. Then the ram got aggressive and came after me.

"Stop!' I yelled, but he kicked me with a lot of force. I fell down on the jagged granite rocks. "OUCH! Help!"

From his hiding place, Apa heard my cries. He ran over to see what had happened. "What happened? Are you okay? EEW!

gross! blood! I'm gonna throw up!" Apa exclaimed, when he saw my bloody left hand and my arm where the bone poked out.

The sheep started to lick the blood. "Don't!" Apa shouted at them. He helped me get up. "We have to get you to the hospital. Can you walk?"

"Yes, but don't touch me!" I held my arm still and close to my body. I felt light-headed and nearly blacked out, the pain was so intense. "I don't know how far I can walk like this. We need help."

Phura Tharkey interrupted my story to say, "I can imagine how painful that must have been. One time, I fractured my arm and the pain was excruciating! How did you get to the hospital?"

Apa saw a neighbor, and called out, "Hey, can you help us?"

"Oh, that looks awful!" he said. "I'll take you to the hospital. I have a wicker chair at my house. It's close by. Apa and I can carry you using that chair."

They carried me on the chair, but it was a rough ride, and every bump sent pain through my arm. It seemed like it took forever to get to the hospital.

When we got there, the doctor asked me, "How did this happen? What were you doing?"

After I told him what had happened, he asked, "How much pain do you feel?"

"It is the worst pain I've ever felt!"

"I'll give you some medication to relieve the pain," the doctor said. "You'll need to stay in the hospital for a few days so the swelling can go down and we can fix your arm."

Uncle, sensing I'd finished my story, commented, "I remember how awful that was! It's amazing that it healed so well." Phura Tharkey nodded in agreement.

As we talked, I heard yaks' bells in the distance. Looking up the hill beyond the stone wall that surrounds the *partetu*, we saw a cloud of dust. The yaks' hooves churned up the dirt as they descended the steep hillside.

Mother followed closely behind them. When she arrived, she was dusty and looked surprised. "What is all this commotion about? Why are you all here instead of doing your chores?" she scolded her children.

I burst out, "Mother, I am going to go see the king of Nepal!"

"You're *what*?" She responded in disbelief.

"Mother," I said, "This is *Hajur* Phura Tharkey, a messenger from the king. He brought a summons for me to appear before the king in his palace in Kathmandu!"

She looked stunned!

Mother brushed the dirt off her black *tongkok* dress, then held her hands in the prayer position and greeted Phura Tharkey with respect. "Namaste. I, Chamba Sherpa, Sonam's mother, am honored to make your acquaintance, *Hajur* Phura Tharkey. Welcome to our village." She made a small bow.

"Namaste. I am pleased to meet you," said Phura Tharkey. "It is impressive to see how much you and Sonam look alike. You both have round faces with chocolate-colored, slanted eyes that reveal your gentle souls. Chamba, your weather worn face shows you have lived the hardships of life in these rocky, cold mountains for many years."

My mother smiled. "Please, do tell me what is happening?"

As Uncle told her what had happened in the past few hours, her mouth dropped open in astonishment.

Phura Tharkey nodded in agreement. "The king has a problem that he needs Sonam to help him solve. He didn't give any details about the problem. He just told me that I need to bring Sonam with me to Kathmandu, and there he will tell Sonam in person what he wants him to do to help solve the problem."

"This is very serious! What can our small, young son possibly do to help the king?" Mother questioned. "Before we can allow him to go with you, we need to consult with Dakshi,

Sonam's father." Then turning to me she asked, "Sonam, how do you think you can help the king?"

"I don't know," I replied, "but if the king needs me, I need to go, don't I?"

Three

Mother, Phura Tharkey, and the family stood on the path near our house and discussed the king's summons. In the background, we heard the yaks grunt and their bells ring as they moved their heads. Family members joined us and came up with various ideas of ways that I might be able to help the king.

Dorje's idea was, "Maybe he wants to raise sheep in the backyard of the palace and wants you to be the shepherd."

Pasang suggested, "Maybe he wants you to play school with his little children, if he has any."

Lakpa chimed in, "Maybe . . . "

Wise Mother interrupted and said, "Before a final decision can be made whether Sonam should go to see the king or not, we need to discuss this with Papa. He is on an expedition so we may not know the answer for a few days. Dorje, go find your father and tell him to return home as soon as possible."

Sixteen-year-old, Dorje, his friends, and a guide would set out immediately because they knew it could take a few days to find Papa on Sagarmatha. Mother encouraged the rest of us to return to the house. She promised that we could show Phura Tharkey the village tomorrow.

On the way back to the house, we passed the Khumjung monastery with its red brick walls decorated with colorful geometric shapes, short golden curtains, and Buddhist art. In the temple was a giant prayer wheel covered with fabric that was three times as tall as I am. Inside the wheel was a roll of paper upon which prayers are written. Every time someone turned the wheel a little bell rang, and the person gained merit.

I told Phura Tharkey, "This is a center for our Sherpa religion and culture. Our father wants Pasang to become a monk. He would study here."

Phura Tharkey asked Pasang, "Would you like to study here and become a monk?"

Pasang frowned. "I think it would be awful sitting inside a dark temple all day reading dusty old writings. I'd rather play outside with my friends. But I would learn to read and that would be good."

"Reading is good. It allows you to learn about a lot of different things," Phura Tharkey responded.

I joined the conversation. "At my school we read about Nepal and places far away. We read about famous people, scientific discoveries, and much more. It's so interesting to learn all those things! I know there is a lot more to learn, and that's why I want to go to secondary school."

Phura Tharkey nodded encouragement.

"My friend, Apa's older brother, went to secondary school," I continued, "while my older brother, Dorje, became a farmer. I prefer to do what Apa's brother did. He's smart and motivated, so his primary teacher inspired him to go to secondary school. I remember he liked to learn about how people live in ways that are different than ours. He also had a class in art where he studied about cave paintings. I would love that class! He did so well in secondary school that he was awarded a scholarship to study at the university!"

Phura Tharkey agreed. "I am so glad that I also got to study at the university. Education is valuable and fun, and more opportunities come to those who are well educated."

"Apa and I both want to go to secondary school, and we hope we can go to the same school. I hope we find an excellent one, and that somehow we can find enough money to pay for it."

As we walked the rest of the way home, we continued our conversation about school and how fun it is to learn new things. When we got home, Grandma made Sherpa stew for dinner. It had many root vegetables—like potatoes, carrots, and turnips—mixed with spinach and thick wheat-flour noodles. She added onions, turmeric, garlic, ginger, and chilis. The sauteed chilis and garlic made a piquant aroma that smelled delicious.

That evening, we sat by the warm fire and listened as Phura Tharkey, in a rich, resonant voice, described his trip from Kathmandu to Khumjung.

"A few weeks ago," he began, "the king commissioned me to take this trip to Khumjung. It took me about two weeks to walk from my home on the palace grounds near where the king lives. I trekked from the elevation of 1400 meters in Kathmandu to Khumjung whose altitude is 3790 meters. I felt fortunate to be chosen to make this journey."

"When I was a child," Phura Tharkey recounted, "I contracted polio and walked with a limp. I thought I would never be able to take long walks. My mother had had severe polio, and her ability to walk was very limited. She couldn't take care of me and my brother. My father, who built roads, had to work and was gone most of the time. My kind uncle, the king, raised us as if we were his own children."

The king is Phura Tharkey's uncle? I thought, *and raised him like a son? A close relative of the king of Nepal seated in our house! How extraordinary!*

Phura Tharkey continued his story, "I am grateful that I am able to walk long distances now and feel privileged that the king gave me the opportunity to do these mountain trips for him. Plus, I have been able to see beautiful places and meet wonderful people."

Phura Tharkey went on to describe the wonders he had seen on his trip to my village: Sparkling rivers that turned prayer wheels, clouds that played hide and seek with high snowy peaks, colorful birds, hairy rodents, and several varieties of trees and flowers, including our national flower, the rhododendron.

"In the spring," Phura Tharkey added, "the flowers drape over the path and create a stunning red canopy that reminds me of fireworks. Under them grow little purplish daphne flowers that smell like lemons."

Entranced by his descriptions, I asked Phura Tharkey, "Will we get to see those things on our trip to Kathmandu?"

He paused to consider my question. "Probably we will see some of them, but it will not be the right time of year to see others."

"One late afternoon, as the sky turned dark," said Phura Tharkey, "I heard blaring sounds that sounded like brass horns. They were so loud I covered my ears, but I was intrigued so I followed the sounds and arrived at a Hindu shrine. There I saw villagers dancing. Some holy men waved flaming lamps while other holy men blew into conch shells that created a piercing sound."

A villager had explained to Phura Tharkey that the ritual is called *Arati* and it is done to honor the deities and remove the darkness.

"At the ceremony I met a sort of wild-looking holy man, a *sadhu*. He had a long, scraggly beard and a turban on his head. His face was painted orange and yellow, and on his forehead was a coin-shaped, red, tika mark made with sandalwood paste. He wore a saffron robe and long necklaces of marigolds, animal bones, and 108 seeds. He was kind and invited me to spend the night with him in his cave, but I was hesitant to accept his invitation."

"Yeah, he sounds a little scary," I said.

"I did stay with a Buddhist monk in his monastery, though," Phura Tharkey responded adding, "Sonam, since your brother Pasang plans to become a monk, I will tell you about that monastery."

"Inside the monastery, monks were engaged in a lot of activity: some meditated and read sacred texts; older monks taught novice monks; they all chanted, accompanied by thunderous drums and long Tibetan horns that sound haunting yet musical."

"It was so loud I thought I would never fall asleep. Some monks had created mandalas and painted colorful paintings called *tankas* on the walls inside the monastery. Sonam, since you like to draw, I think you would have enjoyed those pictures."

Above the monastery, colorful prayer flags attached to tall posts fluttered in the breezes, spreading goodwill and compassion to all living things.

The monks explained. "Each color has a meaning: blue for sky or space, white for air or clouds, red for fire, green for water, yellow for earth. They are always displayed in that order."

"Outside in the stone courtyard, I saw monks dance a wild dance. They wore devilish-looking masks and whirled and jumped to the blaring music."

"It would be funny to see my brother dance like that," I responded.

Phura Tharkey smiled and went on, "Although I was invited to sleep in a cave and a monastery, most nights I slept in a

village inn on a bamboo mat. The innkeepers gave me chai to drink and a simple traditional meal, *dal bhat* and rice. One night I was sound asleep on the porch of an inn when I was startled awake by a growling sound. I felt like something was breathing down my neck. I lay very still as if paralyzed and held my breath until finally the noise went away. I could not see it, but the next morning I saw enormous footprints. It must have been a huge animal!"

"It could have been a Himalayan brown bear, or maybe even a yeti! When I realized how close it had been to me, I was petrified! But also fascinated."

"That's intense!" I quaked.

"The route I took was the same one that mountain climbers take on their way to Sagarmatha. One day I met an Austrian climber named Hans who had golden hair and light skin that reminded me of the beautiful Indian White-eye bird. Hans was on his way back from an expedition up Sagarmatha (which he referred to as Mount Everest) and had many stories to tell. Hans told me he was impressed with the Sherpa who was his guide. The Sherpa guide was from Khumjung so you may know him, but Hans didn't tell me his name."

I was excited and blurted out, "My father is a guide up Sagarmatha! Maybe Hans was one of his climbers!"

Uncle reprimanded me, "Nephew, you must not interrupt *Hajur* Phura Tharkey when he speaks."

But Phura Tharkey responded, "Please do not stop. I would like to learn more about your family."

Uncle Mingma looked at me as if to say, it's okay, go ahead. So now it was my turn to tell a tale.

"My father, Dakshi Sherpa, has been a guide for mountain climbers ever since he was a teenager," I began.

I explained that many Sherpa people are guides and porters, but not all porters and guides are Sherpas. As a novice, my father had apprenticed with Tenzing Norgay, a man from our village who guided Sir Edmund Hillary to the top of our beloved Sagarmatha. They were the first people to climb to the top of the world's highest mountain! They summited at 11:30 in the morning of May 29, 1953, Tenzing Norgay's thirty-ninth birthday.

"My father leads climbers to the 8,848-meter summit of Sagarmatha and teaches novices how to become guides. They use our yaks to carry heavy loads of climbing gear. Once my father brought an Austrian climber to our house. He was a nice man, and we had a good talk but he didn't stay long, and I don't know his name."

The Austrian had asked me, "What do you like to do while your sheep graze?"

"I like to look at the birds and the little animals under the rocks, and I like to try to draw them."

"I like to draw too," The Austrian replied. "I brought some special art paper with me. Would you like some?"

"It would be nice to have special paper." I thanked him in our Sherpa language, "*Thuche*."

"Could you draw a picture for me of your family and your mountainous village so I can take it to my eleven-year-old son?" the blond man asked.

"Yes, I would be glad to. I would like to meet your son. Can you bring him here someday?'"

"That is a nice dream. I will try to make it come true for you."

The Austrian climber gave me pastels and special paper, and in return I drew a picture for him. I drew identical houses, all whitewashed stone with wooden window frames and stone roofs, which I explained were held in place with a paste made of yak droppings and mud. I drew colorful prayer flags, our village monastery, *stupa*, *mani* walls, rocky pathways, and the beautiful high mountains that surround our village. I thought the pictures were very good.

Phura Tharkey commented, "Those must have been very special pictures. I wish I could have seen them. It's true, all the houses do look the same here. When I arrived in Khumjung, it was difficult to find your house. Fortunately, one of your neighbors directed me to your home. Your grandmother was outside and welcomed me. Now your gracious mother has also welcomed me into your home, given me delicious food to eat, and showed me a comfortable place to sleep. I am grateful for all this."

Mother smiled. "It is late now. Pasang and Lakpa are asleep. Let us all settle down for the night." We were about to crawl into our beds when we heard footsteps on the ladder that leads up to the house.

To our astonishment, Dorje and Papa walked in the door. Papa limped. His clothes were dirty and torn, and he appeared very upset.

"Papa, what happened?!"

"There was an avalanche!" Papa explained, "Our team of ten climbers," five men on each rope team, "had just climbed over a perilous frozen wall when we saw a house-sized chunk of ice crash down the mountain! We heard an awful roar and knew an avalanche had been set off. We had to get out of there in a hurry! My team got to camp without any problems, but my assistant guide and four climbers didn't arrive. It was horrible to think they might be buried!"

Papa explained that he and his team immediately rushed to where Papa thought they'd find the missing climbers, dreading to think about whether they had survived!

"To our relief, we found three of the climbers and the assistant guide, shaken but with only a few minor injuries. No one knew where the other climber was. We all searched in a crisscross pattern, digging in the snow to try to find the missing climber. We didn't have much time. We needed help and we needed it fast!"

Seeing that avalanche, Papa got chilled and shaky remembering another time a few years ago when he was buried in an avalanche. He retold the story for Phura Tharkey and me.

"Help! Avalanche!" I had yelled as the quickly moving snow pulled me down into it.

I couldn't get out! I was upside down, no, right side up? I couldn't tell what direction was up, Papa recounted.

I needed to swim to the top of the snow, *but what direction was up?* My body flipped upside down in two somersaults. Everything moved in slow motion. A rock hit my leg and I heard it crack. I thought my leg had been broken.

Pain! I have to swim to the top of the snow!

"Help! . . . My body . . . I can't move . . . " I cried out again.

The snow was as heavy as cement on top of me. My back hit a tree. I knew I had to tuck my head and make an air pocket so I could breathe. It was pitch black under there. My life flashed before my eyes, I thought, *I'm going to die! I have to get my arm up to the top of the snow.*

Arm, go up! You have to go up!

Push hard.

My arm broke the surface of the snow, and I blacked out.

"It must have been only a short time until my friends rescued me," Papa concluded, "because otherwise, I wouldn't have survived. Somehow, they got a helicopter and got me into it. When I awoke, I was in the hospital."

I was almost out of breath just listening to him! "Papa, I am so glad you survived that. Are the people in today's avalanche going to survive too?"

"I hope so!" Papa replied, "I had just left the avalanche site and was on my way to get help when Dorje arrived on the mountainside. Dorje insisted I come home and meet Phura Tharkey, the king's messenger! When I asked Dorje why a messenger from the king had come to Khumjung, he told me about the summons that required him to take Sonam to the palace to meet the king."

"My son, these words you speak are crazy!" Papa had told Dorje.

"Dorje and I moved as quickly as we could, but we had to stop at the guard station and tell them about the avalanche, so they could get a helicopter to rescue the climbers. I'm eager to leave again immediately to go back and help."

Worry lines etched his face as he spoke rapidly to Mother and Uncle, "Chamba, Mingma, why did Dorje come to get me? Who is this man?"

As Uncle repeated the story he had told Mother earlier, Papa calmed down, focusing on each word. As Uncle told of the summons from the king, Papa and Mother exchanged looks of disbelief. I listened to their conversation with Phura Tharkey as they discussed their many concerns.

Papa asked, "Did Sonam do something wrong that the king wants to punish him?"

Phura Tharkey assured Papa, "The king told me he has a problem that he wants Sonam to help him solve, so I am sure he does not plan to punish Sonam."

Mother questioned, "How can our young son help the mighty king solve any problem? He is smart and talented but he's so young. Maybe Dorje should go instead."

Phura Tharkey replied, "I'm sorry, Chamba, but the king summoned Sonam not Dorje."

Mother exclaimed, "This is a bad idea! I don't want him to go. Sonam could get hurt, lost, or kidnapped! If something bad happens to him I'll never forgive myself for letting him go. Who will take care of him if something bad does happen?"

Phura Tharkey assured her "I will take good care of Sonam, and the king's people along the way to Kathmandu will help if need arises, and one of your family members will also accompany us."

Papa spoke. "With all those resources, Sonam should be safe."

But to himself Papa wondered if Phura Tharkey truly was the king's messenger. *Was his story the truth? The summons looked real, but what if it was not? Well at least a family member would be present to keep Sonam safe. And Sonam would get a trip to Kathmandu, which would be educational.* He looked at Mother and said, "If it's real it will be an exciting opportunity. I do want the best for our son."

But Mother worried aloud, "Who will give Sonam food and a place to stay? I'm afraid the king will keep him forever in Kathmandu. When will he come back?"

Phura Tharkey tried to reassure her. "I don't know when he'll return but I promise that the king and his servants will take good care of Sonam and your family member who accompanies him. After we meet with the king, we will be able to answer your question as to how long he'll need to stay in Kathmandu."

Mother turned to Papa. "Dakshi, I am not in favor of this plan. We can't let him go!"

Papa replied "There is a summons from the king. Who are we to question the king? We have to abide by the summons. We have to let him go."

Mother sighed and with resignation said, "I will let him go. I will miss my young son. His absence will make it harder for me and the family. Who will take care of the sheep while he's away? There'll be more work for me. I'll have to take both the yaks and the sheep up to the fields to graze. That will be hard."

Papa said, "We'll have to make things work. Other family members will help you."

Mother fretted, "I hope he doesn't stay away too long."

"I know this will be hard for you," Phura Tharkey sympathized, "but it is good you have arrived at this decision. If Sonam did not obey the summons, the consequences would be quite strong."

Papa and Mother had made their decision. "You must indeed go with Phura Tharkey," Papa told me. "The king has summoned you so you must go. One of the family members will accompany you."

Though I was also nervous about what lay ahead for me, I was delighted with their decision.

Then Papa announced, "Now I must go back to my climbers."

"You are exhausted!" Mother objected. "Sleep a few hours and leave early in the morning."

"It's true I am tired," Papa assented, lamenting "I won't be able to do this work when I am old. It'll be important for Sonam to make a good living so he can support us. The yak wool blankets you make won't earn us enough income to live on. We'll need him to help us. I hope he'll find an excellent secondary school and maybe even go on to the university. Then he'll be able to find good work. Who knows? Maybe this visit to the king will lead to some miracle."

Soon after he said that, he fell sound asleep and snored as loud as a bear.

Early the next morning, as the sky changed from night to day before everyone else was awake, I heard papa readying to leave. I got up, hugged him, and whispered, "Be careful, Papa."

Without a sound Papa tiptoed out of the house to return to the mountain and his injured climbers.

He had gone a few meters when he turned back and called to me, "Sonam, when we were at the summit of Sagamartha, your favorite bird, the gray Bar-Headed Goose, flew over us. It was close enough that we could see its head with its orange beak and two dark black bars. That was incredible!" I was delighted to hear that. I wondered if it was the same bird I had seen yesterday when I was up on the hillside with the sheep. *What a special day that was,* because shortly after I saw the geese, Phura Tharkey arrived with the message from the king for me! *Wow!* But, before I could discuss all that with Papa, he was gone.

Not long after Papa left, we heard *chop, chop, chop, chop.* Outside, we looked up and saw a helicopter. I worried and wondered who was in the helicopter? *Why was it here?*

Four

The helicopter hovered near the hospital.

"Let's go see what's happening!" I exclaimed.

Grandma, Uncle, Mother, Lhakpa, Pasang, Phura Tharkey, and I scurried along the path. We arrived as the helicopter ambulance descended and landed. Dust flew everywhere. We shielded our eyes from the flying debris. The wind from the rotors caused our clothes to flap wildly and the noise was so loud that we covered our ears.

Two doctors and two nurses rushed out from the hospital to meet the helicopter. They were careful not to get hit by its twirling blades as they pulled out two injured climbers with blood-stained clothing, black frostbitten fingers, and pale faces.

The nurses and doctors placed each of the climbers on a padded wooden stretcher. Four porters carried each stretcher from the helipad down the grassy slope, past the stone walls, along the dirt path to the hospital. The climbers were transferred to gurneys and wheeled into the hospital.

One of the doctors looked over and saw me. He was the doctor who had fixed my arm after the ram kicked me the year before.

He stopped for a moment and asked me, "Sonam, how's your left arm?"

"There's a little scar on my arm and one of my fingers is stiff, but otherwise I am fine. I can draw pictures without any problems."

"I'm so glad your arm and hand have healed well. Your artwork is wonderful, and I'd hate for you not to be able to draw." Then he ran off to care for the climbers.

Uncle then told Phura Tharkey, "We are fortunate that Sir Edmund Hillary gave us the hospital and the two-room schoolhouse. Khumjung is the only community in our region that has a hospital and a school."

Grandmother added, "Sir Hillary never could have made it to the top of Sagarmatha without our Tenzing Norgay. To honor him and Khumjung, Sir Hillary paid to have the hospital and school built. He visits Khumjung once or twice a year.

"When he comes," Uncle commented, "He flies into the airfield at Lukla. Sherpas from our village helped him build that airfield."

Pasang added, "When he comes to visit, we hold a big festival for him in the schoolyard."

"Let's go now and see the school that Sir Hillary built for us and the place where festivals are held," I urged Phura Tharkey and my family.

As we walked toward the school, I told Phura Tharkey about my school's art project. Students had made paper mâché masks, carvings, baskets, and drawings. One student had woven a small carpet. When we arrived at the school, I opened the door of the classroom and was pleasantly surprised to see the artwork creatively displayed on the walls and on top of the barren wooden benches that we use for our desks.

I was especially excited to see the Ganesh statue a fellow student had sculpted. I told Phura Tharkey, "I really like Ganesh.

Ganesh is the Hindu elephant god of learning and art. Even though I am Buddhist, I think Ganesh helps me a lot."

Noticing that the Ganesh statue had been awarded second place, I wondered what art piece might have been awarded first place? We looked at each entry on the desks then looked at the art on the wall where my drawing and other drawings were exhibited.

"Wow!" I exclaimed with joy.

Next to my drawing was the blue ribbon. *I won first place in the art show!* I was sure Ganesh had helped me win the award. My family and I were all so delighted! When Phura Tharkey congratulated me, a warm feeling of pride came over me.

Within a short time, the room was filled with people. Everyone stared at me. I felt my face warm with embarrassment. Many other people looked in through the windows and the doorway. I thought it was because I'd been awarded the blue ribbon, so I stood a little taller and smiled.

Then I heard whispers. "I can't see him. Does he have a crown on his head?"

"What's he look like?"

"Can we go up and talk to him?"

"What's his name? Is he really a messenger from the king?"

Word had spread like wildfire throughout the community that a messenger from the king was here. I wanted to hide when I realized the mistake I had made thinking they wanted to see me, the winner of the art show. I felt a bit disappointed that they didn't want to honor me for my artwork, yet I also felt relieved that I was not the object of their stares. I recovered my dignity and pride when I realized if it weren't for me, the king's messenger wouldn't be here.

Teacher Pemba quieted the crowd and, in her gentle voice, instructed everyone, "Go outside to the open field in front of the school. Phura Tharkey, the king's messenger, will greet us there."

As they moved outside, Teacher Pemba told Phura Tharkey "This is the first art show we've ever had. Fifteen of the forty students in the school created objects of art. That's a great accomplishment. I am proud of each one of them. I am also pleased to tell you that Sonam, the winner of first place, is our brightest student. I predict he will go far in life."

Grandmother overheard what Teacher Pemba had said to Phura Tharkey. She gushed, "Sonam's parents and I are very proud of how smart and talented Sonam is. His father, Dakshi, chose him to be the educated son. Dakshi understands the value of education and would love to be able to send Sonam to an excellent school in Kathmandu, though he knows that's a wild dream. Dakshi trusts that he and Sonam's mother, Chamba, will be cared for in their old age since Sonam is so smart and talented."

"Papa thinks I should become a business owner someday" I explained to Phura Tharkey. "He imagines me having a little shop on the main road in Khumjung. But I don't want to own a business. I'd rather be a scientist or a doctor or an artist or something else, not a businessman."

Phura Tharkey understood. "You are young, you don't have to know at this time what you want. Your father seems like a wise man. Trust him to help you figure that all out when you need to. It is good to know that you do well in school and are a talented artist. Please tell me about your blue-ribbon drawing."

"I used the pastels and some of the special paper that the Austrian climber gave me. It took me a few days to complete the picture. First, I practiced drawing the sheep that I spend time with on the hillside every day after school, next I drew a landscape and placed my sheep in it. Then I drew a final copy of that."

Phura Tharkey asked, "Did anyone teach you how to draw?"

"No, I taught myself. I love to look at the details of things— rocks, sheep, bugs, and everything around me. People tell me that I see things that no one else sees. It surprises me when they say that!"

In the open field outside the school, a huge group of villagers gathered. They were all curious to hear the king's messenger, but I was to speak first to introduce Phura Tharkey and explain why he was sent to Khumjung.

I stood as tall as possible, and in my most grown-up voice I told the villagers, "The king sent his messenger, Phura Tharkey, to Khumjung to deliver a summons. It says 'Sonam Sherpa is to appear before the king in the palace in Kathmandu to help the king solve a problem.'"

The crowd erupted in disbelief. I heard various voices saying, "That can't be true!"

"Such delusions of grandeur you have, peasant boy! What could you do to help the king?"

"You made this up! How does the king even know you exist?"

"That man probably isn't *really* the king's messenger."

I felt hurt that they didn't believe me, but *I* knew what I said was true. *The king did want my help.* At least I thought it was true. *But what if they were right? What if it was all a farce?* Phura Tharkey seemed so honest; it must be true.

As soon as Phura Tharkey began to speak, the crowd stopped jeering and, with eyes wide open, they listened to every word he had to say.

"I bring you greetings from King Birendra Bir Bikram Shah Dev. He sent me here, to Khumjung, to meet Sonam Sherpa, his family, and you, the people of Khumjung."

I could see the villagers stood a little taller and prouder.

"The king issued a summons for Sonam to return with me to Kathmandu to meet with his Majesty." Gasps could be heard from the surprised crowd.

"The king told me he has a problem that Sonam can help him solve, but I do not know what the problem is, nor how an eleven-year-old peasant boy from Khumjung can solve it for him. For King Birendra to summon Sonam Sherpa is a significant honor. Not only for Sonam and his family but for your whole community!"

Now with bright, twinkling eyes, the people showed their pride and gratitude. They smiled and elbowed each other.

"King Birendra is a benevolent king and a loving father. He is a smart, kind, humble, cultured man, who writes poetry and appreciates and collects art. He would have loved to see the art show with all the fine pieces that Khumjung's students have created."

The student artists nodded and smiled at each other.

"The king works hard on behalf of the people of the kingdom!" Phura Tharkey intoned. "He makes sacrifices so that the citizens can have schools, hospitals, good clean drinking water, and roads. But due to the terrain, it's hard to provide those things for everybody."

"In the northern Himal region are the extremely high Himalaya mountains. In the middle Pahad (hilly) region are lower mountains, hills and valleys. And in the southern Terai region are grasslands and a steamy jungle."

"It's a big challenge to govern all the people, especially since 123 different languages are spoken in the kingdom. King

Birendra loves to travel, and I know he would love to be here with you. But it takes all his time to do the things a monarch must do: he creates laws that protect the environment and laws that help farmers and other groups; he works with people from many countries and attends ceremonies. He is revered and loved by the people of Nepal and the world!"

Finally Phura Tharkey closed with a quote from King Birendra himself: "I shall remain alert and active for the sake of my country. I shall be my people's beloved . . . May we all remain alert and active for the sake of our country!'"

As Phura Tharkey spoke I looked around and noticed a man in the crowd who was dressed in baggy white pants. He was not from Khumjung. *Where is he from and why is he here? I*

wondered. He stared with an intense, sinister look right at my little sister, Lakpa, so I moved over and stood beside her. The man seemed to notice and disappeared.

When Phura Tharkey finished his presentation, the astonished, exhilarated crowd erupted into a festive mood. Rhythmic songs and dancing feet created an exuberant, instantaneous celebration.

Someone picked me up and tossed me into the air. They passed me from person to person.

The festivities continued and this time they focused on me!

At the end of the celebration, the mayor of our village placed a scarf, a *khata*, around my neck and another one around Phura Tharkey's neck.

People in the crowd offered me many blessings.

Mother hugged me and whispered in my ear, "You look so happy. Your big brown eyes sparkle, and your smile reaches from ear to ear."

Our village's Buddhist *lama* bade me, "Travel with the gods. Be fully present wherever you are. Empty your mind of expectations."

My father's climbing partner wished me, "Have a safe journey. Enjoy every step!"

Our kind, next-door-neighbor lady advised me, "Express gratitude. Share your happiness. Be open to changes."

Apa's father counselled, "Show respect to the king, and his messenger. May you solve the king's problem."

Apa whispered, "I'll miss you, buddy."

With great curiosity, the mayor begged, "As soon as you know, send word of how you can solve this kingly problem!"

Phura Tharkey expressed his gratitude for their good wishes and informed everyone, "The king wants us to arrive in Kathmandu in three days. In order to fulfill the wishes of the king, we must depart early in the morning."

With trepidation Mother whispered to Grandmother, "They'll leave so soon! Sonam is so young to do this! What if something bad happens to him?"

Five

We hurried home to make preparations for the next day's departure. Grandma prepared potato pancakes and dumplings for us to take on our trip and *dal bhat* for the evening's dinner. The kitchen smelled of warm bread, spicy dumplings, and savory *dal bhat*. It whetted my appetite.

Mother helped me decide which of my meager belongings I should take on this grand journey to Kathmandu. I decided to take the special paper and pastels the Austrian climber had given me so that I could draw pictures of things I'd see along the way. She gave me a copper box with a lid to carry the special paper in, so it would stay dry if it rained. I put the box and all my things into a waterproof bag. I put them inside my small green backpack, a gift that one of the climbers had given me.

Mother encouraged me, "Be sure to draw pictures of your trip so that you can show them to our family and friends when you return."

I was nervous and full of excitement, disbelief, and questions. *Why does the king want me, a poor peasant boy, to help him? What can I wear to visit the king? I have no special clothes. What gift should I take to the king? I have nothing of value to present to him. Who will take care of the sheep while I'm gone? Who will go with me and Phura Tharkey?*

I wished Papa could go with me, but he had to teach novices how to become climbing guides. Since Papa couldn't go, Grandma and Mother agreed Papa's brother, Uncle Mingma, would be the best family member to go with me. I was glad he agreed to go because he's my favorite uncle.

Uncle was excited but a bit anxious. "This will be an exciting once-in-a-lifetime experience, and I'm glad I get to go with you. Yet, I hope it won't take long because Sir Edmund Hillary plans to visit Khumjung in a few months, and I want to build a house for him before he arrives. He has done so much for our community, so I want to make a special place for him to stay when he visits Khumjung."

The following day everyone in the family got up early in the morning to send us off. Excitement was in the air. However, it was a bitter cold, windy morning so we decided to delay our departure for a few hours. My brothers and sister grumbled, their moods reflecting the weather.

Dorje expressed his frustration, "Why was Sonam chosen to go? What makes him so special? I'm the oldest son. It should be me who gets to go to meet the king and see the capital city."

Pasang complained, "It's not fair. Sonam is going to leave, and I have to stay here with my hands in the yak's poop. Plus, I'll have to do more chores since he'll be gone."

Lakpa whined, "I don't want Sonam to go. I'll miss him. When he's not here, who will help me carry the potatoes to market?"

"Children, children, stop your grumbling," Mother scolded. "Different experiences come to each person in life. Maybe someday something special will come to you too. But until then, let's wish Sonam a safe and happy experience, and let's speak with the king's messenger while he is here with us."

We turned to Phura Tharkey, many questions on our tongues.

My brothers and sister begged, "Can we go too? We want to see the king!"

Phura Tharkey replied, "No not all the way to Kathmandu, but if you want you can come to the top of the hill with us and send us off from there."

They hurried to get their jackets while Uncle checked his belongings.

When we were ready to leave, Mother and Grandmother each placed a *khata* around my neck and gave me a little squeeze.

Mother reminded me, "Act properly when you meet the King. Be good to your uncle. Be respectful of elders. Be sure to eat well."

They then placed *khatas* around the necks of Uncle and Phura Tharkey, and offered a prayer for our safe journey.

Uncle Mingma and Phura Tharkey put their hands together, bowed slightly and expressed their thanks. Uncle said "*thuche*" and Phura Tharkey said "*dhanyabad.*"

My brothers, Dorje and Pasang, and my sister, Lakpa, walked with us for the first part of our trek. The wind chilled our teeth and sounded like a river rushing against our ears. We were glad we had warm jackets to protect us. We walked through the village past the potato fields with their meter high stone walls. We turned the prayer wheels as we passed the *chorten* with its flapping prayer flags. Then we passed the long *mani* wall where we chanted the prayer words *om mani padme hum.*

We left the village and climbed the big rock steps up to the top of the hill. When we arrived at the top, the air was still and there were no clouds in the sky. The warmth of the sun on our backs resonated with the warmth we felt in our hearts for our mountains and village. We gazed for a long time at the many beautiful, sacred, mountains that rise 6000 meters above Khumjung. Mountains teach us about life with its peaks and valleys; that is why we consider them sacred. We could see six mountains:

Tabuche looks like a dog's sharp tooth.

Sagarmatha is the world's highest mountain.

Lhotse looks like the thirteen steps that lead to enlightenment on the *chorten*.

Thamserku looks like a big smile with a peak on each end of the U.

Kongde Ri is a ridge with multiple summits.

And majestic Ama Dablam, whose name means "Mother's necklace," because the long ridges on each side are like arms of an *ama,* a mother, protecting her child. The mountain's hanging glacier is thought of as the *dablam,* a pendant that a Sherpa woman wears around her neck.

I told my brothers and sister, "It's time for you to go back home now. We need to continue our walk so we can arrive in Namche Bazaar before dark."

Sadly they said, "Good bye, Phura Tharkey, Uncle and Sonam. Have a good journey and greet King Birendra for us."

We walked a short distance past the helicopter landing pad in Syangboche, then continued to the top of the ridge overlooking Namche Bazaar. Looking down its steep sides, we saw a village, that looked tiny in the bowl-shaped cirque below. The long, dusty, rocky trail wound steeply down from Syangboche to Namche Bazaar.

As Uncle, Phura Tharkey and I descended towards Namche Bazaar, I spotted caves on the hillside. "Can we go and look in those caves to see if there are any cave paintings in them? If there are, maybe they are in better condition than the one in the cave on Mt Khumbila."

"I'll go with you, let's hurry," Uncle said. We ran over and looked inside the caves, then ran back to join Phura Tharkey.

Uncle told him, "Too bad we didn't see any cave paintings."

"Someday I hope I get to see some excellent ones," I said.

Phura Tharkey encouraged us to walk fast, "We must walk quickly to get to my cousin's house before the sun sets. We won't be able to find our way there in the dark."

When we arrived, it wasn't dark at all! Candles glittered in the windows of some of the houses. We saw red-powder designs, marigolds and footprints. I wondered where the footprints led and began to follow some of them.

Phura Tharkey stopped me, "Do not walk there. Those are made for Laxmi, not for you."

"Who is Laxmi?" I asked.

"She is the Hindu goddess of wealth and prosperity. She has four arms. Hindu people believe that she brings them prosperity. That is why we clean and decorate our houses, put-up lights, make a path of footprints, and leave our doors open in the evening—so she can find her way into our homes," Phura Tharkey explained that he and his cousins were Hindu.

It felt like a good sign to arrive in Namche Bazaar during this festival, especially when I learned my favorite god Ganesh, the god of wisdom and wealth, was being honored along with Laxmi.

"Why do the cows wear marigold necklaces, and why do they have red marks on their foreheads and little red flags on their tails?" I asked Phura Tharkey.

He explained, "In our religion, people worship cows. We think of a cow as mother since we grow up drinking her milk. Most of the people in Namche Bazaar are Buddhist like you, but it's hard to tell our two religions apart because they have merged in so many ways."

"Listen!" I heard kids singing. "What is that song? Look! Some kids are playing stringed instruments, *sarangis*. How wonderful that we arrived here during a festival!"

When we got closer, some boys called to me, "Hey, do you want to come with us?"

"Where are you going?" I asked.

"We go from house to house and sing a song called 'Deusi' so people give us sweets and money. It's a lot of fun."

"Yes, I want to go with you, but I don't know the song," I responded.

"It's simple; we'll teach it to you."

I couldn't sing very well, but that didn't seem to matter. I had fun with the boys, and I even got some money! *I will save the money and use it towards my school expenses*, I vowed.

I noticed that all the boys were younger than me. I wondered why there were no older boys. I asked the boys, and they told me that the older boys were in secondary school, so they had to leave Namche Bazaar and go to another village for school. I wondered, *Might I go to that school, if I can find enough money?*

When we arrived at Phura Tharkey's cousins' house, they welcomed us, "*Namaste*. We are so glad to see you."

They gave each of us a *khata* and delicious *sel roti* to eat. "Tonight is *the* 4th night of Diwali, the five-day Festival of Lights, so we get to eat *sel roti*. Want to see how they are made?"

"Yes, I would like to learn how to make them," Uncle said, so we all went into the kitchen where a woman showed us how to make *sel roti*.

"First," she said, "I heat oil in this copper pot. Then I make a thin batter with wheat flour, rice, butterfat, cardamom and sugar. I pour it through a small funnel into the hot oil. I make it into the shape of a ring. It cooks for a few minutes and then it is ready to eat."

"I'm glad we arrived on the 4th day of Diwali. The warm, sweet, *sel roti* are so tasty!" I said.

The girls in the family told us, "The fifth day of the festival is another special day because we perform a little ritual. We apply red *tika* to our brother's forehead, like the cows have, so Brother will have a long life and continue to protect us. It's our way to say thank you. Want to see how we do it?"

"Okay," I replied.

They applied the red tika to my forehead, and it tickled my face. It made me burst out in laughter, and they laughed too. We all laughed together for a while. That was a lot of fun.

The next day was market day, so we got up early before sunrise. The air was freezing cold. I wore a long-sleeved undershirt, a wool sweater, a warm coat, and a wool scarf, but still I felt a chill and my feet were cold.

The town was abuzz with activity. Traders and vendors came from near and far away to sell their wares at the Saturday bazaar. People also came from all over to shop at the market.

Uncle and Phura Tharkey needed to buy supplies for our trip. We snaked through crowds of people and admired the products

of traders and vendors. They sold everyday necessities such as household items, clothing, copper teapots, special knives, and food.

In the food section was a place that sold mounds of aromatic, pleasant smelling spices. I asked the vendor to tell me about them.

"People cook with them, and they all have some medicinal value as well," the man explained. He also showed me the dried fruits and nuts that he sold: figs, dates, red raisins, cashews, and pistachios. "Would you like to taste some?" he offered.

"Oh yes, *thuche*. Could I try a little of each one?"

"That's a good way to know which ones you'd like to buy."

In another section of the market another vendor sold jewelry and colorful hand knotted carpets, made by Tibetan refugees. The jewelry was made of turquoise and red coral. I looked at the red coral and wondered aloud, "Where did this come from?"

The merchant heard me and explained, "The coral comes from the Mediterranean Sea, a big ocean far away from Nepal. Since Nepal is a landlocked country, I wonder if you know what an ocean is?"

"I've seen pictures of one. It looks like a gigantic lake."

"That's right."

Admiring the rich coral and turquoise, I raved, "This jewelry is beautiful! I wish I could buy some for my mother! But I need to save my money to pay for school," I apologized.

Much to my surprise and joy, the kind merchant gave me a small turquoise and coral pendant to give to Mother. I carefully handed it to Uncle. "Please keep this beautiful pendant safe until I can give it to Mother."

The merchant wished me well. "I hope you are able to go on to an excellent secondary school. It's so valuable to get well educated."

"*Thuche, Thuche,*" I replied.

We continued to walk through the bazaar, and I was glad to find a vendor who sold Tibetan Buddhist objects. We looked at the prayer flags, prayer wheels, conch shell trumpets, saffron incense, and medicines made of animal parts said to have magical curative powers. I saw dehydrated squiggly seahorses, musk deer glands, and rhinoceros horns.

I was intrigued by another vendor and asked about his baggy white pants and the unusual fruits and vegetables he sold.

"My pants are called *dhoti* and where I live, in the *Terai* in southern Nepal, the temperature often goes above 35 degrees Celsius in the summer. There *dhotis* are more comfortable than pants like you wear."

"They do look comfortable," I agreed. "The fruits and vegetables you sell are different than ones we have in Khumjung. They look interesting to me. Please tell me about them."

He pointed to them as he spoke. "The yellow prickly fruits with the green, waxy, tough leaves at the top are called pineapples. They are sweet and tart. These are rambutans," he said, pointing. They were small, red and looked soft but with hairy spines sticking out from the skin. "Inside they are white and creamy," he explained, to my surprise. "They taste sweet and a little sour. Custard apples have little green pillows that protrude from outside and white pulp inside. They are sweet and have small black seeds inside."

"What's that shiny, purple, oblong thing?" I asked.

"That's called eggplant. We must cook that to eat it."

"Is it okay with you if I stay here and draw them?" I asked.

I told Uncle and Phura Tharkey, "I want to stay here and draw this vendor with his unique pants and fruits and vegetables. They're colorful and the textures and shapes are different from anything we have. Also, they are displayed in a creative way. Can I please stay here?"

They hesitated. Then Uncle cautioned, "It's not safe for you to be here alone. We're not from here, and no one knows you."

"I'll stay right here by the vendor," I promised.

They discussed the plan with the vendor and finally agreed to let me stay. "Okay, you can stay *but don't go anywhere else. We only need to buy a couple more things. We will return soon.*"

I sat down and got out my special paper that the climber had given me, and I drew the red rambutans. I was absorbed in my drawing until I heard angry voices and saw that the vendor was in an argument with a customer. Their loud voices bothered me until they moved away to look at some merchandise another vendor had. Then the noise of the marketplace, the people milling around, the haggling over prices, the children crying . . . all of it faded away as I got lost in my work.

I had almost completed my third drawing when a strong gust of wind blew my papers away. I jumped up and chased after them.

Then I heard a girl cry out, "Help!"

I looked around and saw a girl who was about my age. The strong wind had pushed over some of the neighboring vendor's heavy boxes, and they had landed on her leg. She couldn't get up. No one else went to help her, so I ran over.

"Take these boxes off my leg!" She pleaded.

I picked up the heavy boxes and put them back in the vendor's area.

"My leg hurts," she said as she rubbed it. It took a lot of effort for her to stand, but she was able to do it without help. She told me her name was Amrita. "Thank you for your help," she sighed. "What is your name?"

"Sonam." I picked up the bars of soap that had scattered when the wind blew them off her tarp where she had displayed them.

"These smell sweet, like flowers," I commented.

"That's because some are made with lavender oil and others with vanilla, mixed with fresh yak milk and red clay. My mother taught me how to make them."

"Oh yes, mothers are good for teaching," I agreed. "My mother taught me how to make blankets from yak wool. It's a long process, but I can do some of it while I tend the sheep."

"How can you weave blankets while tending sheep?" Amrita asked, looking at me as if she wondered if I were a magician or a liar.

"First, we shear the yak, then wash and dry the wool and sort the fibers. Then we spin the yarn on a drop spindle and twist it into a skinny yarn shape. That's the part I do while I tend the sheep. We use the yarn to weave the wool into a blanket or a shawl."

"I've seen yak wool shawls with lovely colors! How do you dye the wool?" Amrita asked.

"We gather plants and use them to dye the wool. It's fun to see the colors change as they soak."

As we talked, I noticed a man staring at her. He was dressed in a *dhoti* like the one worn by the kind vendor from Terai, which seemed unusual around her. I wondered if they knew each other. He had a package under his arm, and looked a bit familiar. *Could this be the same man I saw in Khumjung who stared at my sister and me?*

I motioned with my head in the direction of the man and asked Amrita, "Do you know that man?"

She shook her head, "I don't, though he says he's a friend of my aunt. He makes me nervous. He didn't even tell me his name."

"Are you here alone?"

"Yes," she said her eyes downcast. Sometimes my aunt comes and helps, but she's busy today.

"Where are your parents?"

Little tears formed in her eyes. "They died a year ago in that big earthquake. I live with my aunt."

A shadow crossed her face when she mentioned her aunt. "Do you like living with her?"

She shrugged and paused, maybe wondering how much to say to a strange boy she just met. "She doesn't feed me much," she said quietly, "and she won't let me go to school."

"That's awful!" I replied. I looked at the man again and felt like a girl alone might need some help.

"Amrita, I have to hurry back to the fruit stand. I told my uncle I wouldn't leave there. Let's move your tarp and soaps over there too. Maybe that man won't bother you if we're together and with the kind vendor from Terai."

But the scary man came over to offer his help when Amrita hobbled as we moved the tarp.

Was it kind of him to offer to help? He seems sort of strange, with his weird clothes and accent. Why did he stare at us and not introduce himself to us? Why hadn't Amrita's aunt told her about the man if he was a friend? We looked at him and then looked at each other with quizzical expressions. I wished Uncle were here to help us.

Then the man spoke to me. "I watched you draw. You are a talented artist."

I liked the compliment, *but why he had watched me?* I felt suspicious of him.

"I'm also an artist," the man continued. "I have some of my paintings here with me, because I want to sell them at the market. Would you like to see them?"

No! "No, thank you."

What I really wanted was to continue my drawing, and I was anxious Uncle would be back to the vendor's soon. But the man set down his box and unwrapped his drawings to show me, even though I'd said no.

I saw something shiny in his box! He covered it up quickly so I didn't know what it was, but I was curious.

To my surprise, I liked his paintings—landscapes with animals and people like my drawing that won the art contest. That made me feel more at ease with him.

Then I heard Amrita moan and saw that her face was contorted with pain.

Hearing her, the man offered, "You seem to be in a lot of pain. I know a healer, and I can take you to see her so she can treat your leg injury. I'm sure your aunt would want me to do that."

"How far is it?" Amrita sounded worried.

"It's not far from here. I'll help you walk and maybe Sonam can help too. Sonam, will you help Amrita?"

How can I help her? Uncle told me not to leave here. I don't know this man or Amrita. Uncle will be worried if he comes back and I'm not here. What was that shiny thing in his box that he covered up? He seemed nice now, but what if he wasn't?

Amrita moaned loudly.

Why couldn't the merchant whose boxes fell on her help her? No one seemed to be available. Everyone was busy selling or buying things. I looked around to see if I could find Uncle anywhere, but I didn't. I felt obliged to help Amrita and the friend of her aunt, since they'd asked me. *Uncle would want me to help a person in need*, I thought. *I won't be gone long.*

I packed up my special paper and art supplies, and helped Amrita pack up her belongings. Then I offered to carry her things for her when she again cried out in pain. The man offered his arm to her for support.

On our way to the healer's place, we wound our way through the market. We inhaled smells of sweet juicy oranges mingled with bodily odors of sweaty porters and dung from the mules. After we left the market and traversed the barren hillside, dark clouds formed in the sky above and the path beneath our feet became rough. Our pace was slow because Amrita limped and grimaced with each step.

The only people we saw were two women pulling on ropes that were around the necks of yaks.

As we walked, the man and I talked about art. We talked about how to draw things we saw along the trail. He told me "I know where there are some ancient cave paintings at a cave near the healer's place. The details of the animals and people are in outstanding condition."

That piqued my interest. "Once I saw some cave paintings in a cave by Khumjung, but they were quite faint. I would love to see some with clearly defined details!"

"You would like these. We could stop at that cave and see the paintings."

"Oh yes, I would like that a lot."

We were so engaged in our conversation about the cave paintings, it jolted me out of my thoughts when Amrita whimpered and groaned, "How much farther is it?"

Only then did I realize we had walked quite a distance and weren't even on the main trail anymore. *Had we seen any other people besides those two yak herders since we left the market?*

Now the man's voice was less kind. "It's not far. If you walk faster, we'll get there sooner," the man scolded Amrita.

"I can't walk faster! You told us the healer's place was *near* the market!"

"This *is* taking more time than you told us it would," I affirmed. "My Uncle will be upset when he returns and I'm not where I told him I'd stay. I have to go back!" I spoke firmly to the man, but my mind was racing *I must go back now!*

He grabbed my wrist, swore at us, and ordered, "Keep Walking!"

My muscles tensed. My stomach ached. *I was trapped.*

Six

We weren't safe. Uncle would be upset. He'd wonder where I was.

"I have to go back! I must go back now!" I yelled at our captor.

"No!" he insisted. "It's not far!" then calmly added, "and I am sure you will love the cave paintings . . . and we need to get Amrita to the healer. We need to walk faster."

I wanted to run away. There probably was no healer, and I feared what that silver thing in his box of drawings might be that the man had hidden from my view.

Amrita moaned again from the pain in her leg. I looked for places to escape. There was no place to hide—no trees, no big rocks, only barren hillside.

The man held my wrist so tight it felt like my hands were in handcuffs. He forced me to move in front of him. I twisted and turned and tried to get free, but he held on even tighter. Finally, we got to the cave. It was dark and dank, and there weren't paintings anywhere that I could see.

We have to get out of here! I tried to kick the mean man so he'd let go of me, but instead he grabbed my shoulder and forced me down to the rocky ground.

Then my Uncle's warning flashed through my mind. *You are not safe here. You are not from here and no one knows you.*

I tried to get up, but the frightening man put his foot firmly on my chest and I couldn't move.

"Ow! Help! Leave me alone! Let me out of here!" I yelled,

We had to escape! I shook with fear. I remembered the two rocks that I always carried in my pocket ever since I had to fight off the wolf, but I couldn't get to them with his foot on my chest.

He tried to force Amrita down at the same time. She screamed!

When Amrita wiggled he had to lift his foot off my chest to try to control her, I bolted up and reached in my pocket!

I took out one of the rocks, the one with the sharp pointed tip. Grabbing at his pant leg, I yanked it up and scraped the rock forcefully down the side of his leg. Blood squirted out!

Our captor cried out in pain and grabbed his bleeding leg.

I jumped up! I saw the light at the entrance of the cave and bolted for it.

Amrita, now freed, ran too, crying out in agony each time her foot hit the ground.

The awful man's injured leg prevented him from chasing us. Snarling, he reached into his pocket. That's when I saw the silver thing he had had hidden in his box of drawings. It was a knife!

Terrified, I reached for the second rock in my pocket and got ready to throw it at his eyes.

At that moment, I heard a sound: *click, click, click.*

On the rocky ground outside the cave, someone was running toward us!

Two women appeared in the mouth of the cave. They looked strong! And each held a rope in her hands!

The two women grabbed our captor's arms, forcing him to drop his knife. Then they tied his hands behind his back and his legs together with their ropes.

As he thrashed, one of the women yelled, "Kids help us hold him down! Don't let him get away!"

Amrita and I held down his legs, while the women held down his shoulders. One woman called to a third friend who had waited outside the cave. "Run back to the town and get the police! Hurry!"

We were stuck inside that disgusting cave for a long time, in constant fear that the awful man would get loose before the police arrived. Finally, three policemen arrived, handcuffed the man, and two of the policemen led him away.

The third policeman stayed and talked with all of us. "You did a great service! You secured and held down that man until we arrived!"

"That must have been frightening for you children, but we are fortunate you helped us capture him. He abducted other children before you. Then to me and Amrita he added, Thank you for your help! Now, please tell me your names and tell me what happened."

After we'd told him the whole story, the policeman turned to the two women who had stayed with us. "It's so fortunate that you heard these children and came just in time to save them!"

"We're glad we could help," one woman replied.

The other woman said, "We'll take Sonam and Amrita back to the fruit vendor's market stall and be sure they reconnect with their guardians."

"Are you angels?" I declared, as soon as we were walking. "You set us free! How'd you know we needed help? Where'd you come from?"

"You passed us on the trail after you left the market," one explained.

"You saw us struggling with our yaks, and we saw you with that man," said the other. "We had a sense that something might be wrong so we followed you at a distance. When we heard your cry for help, we ran into the cave."

"You saved our lives!" Amrita and I exclaimed in unison.

When we arrived back at the fruit vendor's place, we saw Uncle and Phura Tharkey pacing back and forth, their brows furrowed. The vendor told us they'd asked all the other vendors, "Did you see where our boy went? Did he go with anyone?" And to those who affirmed they had begged, "What direction did he go?"

When Uncle saw me, he ran over and gave me a big hug. But then he gave me a lecture. "Why did you leave? We trusted you to stay right here. We came back after just a few minutes, and you were not here! What happened to you? Are you ok? We were so worried!"

I told him the whole story of what had happened to us. Then I introduced Uncle and Phura Tharkey to Amrita.

"I was afraid that you had disappeared, and we'd never see you again!" Phura Tharkey replied.

Then the women introduced themselves. One said, "We have received special training to help children when they are in trouble. Amrita, we will go with you back to your aunt's house. There we'll teach you and your aunt how to keep you safe and healthy, how you can get an education, and where you can get help if you need it."

"*Thuche*!" Amrita cried gratefully.

As Amrita prepared to leave, I said, "Good luck with everything. Be careful."

"Thank you, I hope all goes well for you too," Amrita replied.

We helped Amrita pack up her soaps and tarp and said good bye as she left with the women.

Uncle said firmly, "You were lucky those women were there. After this, you can never stay by yourself. You must always be with us!"

"If those women hadn't been there, I could have been stuck in that cave or taken far away like other children the policeman told us about! I'd never go to secondary school. That would be terrible!"

It was good we were in Namche Bazaar during Diwali. Ganesh took care of me. Good did triumph over evil, and I was given a new chance to live!

"I am glad you are safe!" Phura Tharkey said. "How would I have explained to the King that you had disappeared and been kidnapped?!"

Children kidnapped from markets during festivals! That must be a huge problem for the king!! I don't think I can help him solve that problem. I do wonder what problem he has that he thinks I can solve.

I asked Phura Tharkey if we could leave Namche Bazaar as soon as possible, "but first can we get something in the market that will keep the evil spirits away? I don't want my good luck to turn into bad luck."

Phura Tharkey suggested we buy saffron incense; he believed this would both keep the evil spirits away and also bring us good luck. So we went to the Tibetan Buddhist shop, bought some incense, lit it, and carried it with us as we departed Namche Bazaar.

I thought, *now* we will be safe at last!

But as we left town, rain fell, and the wind blew.

Seven

As we left Namche Bazaar, drops of water fell from the branches of the pine trees and rhododendrons and formed small puddles on the pathway. We had fun as we splashed each other in the puddles. We thought it would soon pass over, but much to our surprise, it got worse. It turned into a torrential downpour. The mud, like suction cups, grabbed my feet and pulled me downward.

"Yuck, I'm soaking wet, and my shoes are covered in mud!" I moaned.

"Be careful," Uncle told me, "The wet rocks in the trail are slippery. Walk Slowly. *Slowly*!"

"I know! You don't have to tell me that." I said under my breath.

But just then Uncle slipped and slid several meters down the steep slope. "Help!" he yelled.

I reached out to grab him, but then we both slid further in the soft, slippery mud.

"Ouch," I cried out as thorns on a bush scratched me.

"Aaaaaargh!" we both yelled, panicking.

"We'll get swept down into that deep gorge!" Uncle exclaimed.

"Ow," My foot hit a rock, and I crashed face down into the mud. It felt slimy in my nose, mouth, and hair—and all over my clothes! It was treacherous. "I can't breathe. I'm gonna die!"

Uncle recovered his footing. He pulled me up, looked at me, and laughed.

"It's not funny!" I whimpered.

Uncle said, "You look like a muddy *yeti!*" He laughed some more. It made me mad!

"That incense and Ganesh didn't help me at all!" I complained.

"But maybe Ganesh did keep you safe," Phura Tharkey said, "because you didn't get swept over the rocky ledge."

Uncle wiped the mud off my face and my clothes. "We have to go on. We can't stop here on the edge of this hillside; it could slide down with us on it."

Squish, squish. Mud sloshed in our shoes as we plodded along. Every time I took a step, I was afraid I would slip and fall again. It took a long time to go a short distance.

Finally, Phura Tharke stopped by a big rock with a protective overhang. "We can take a rest under here for a few minutes. It'll provide a good place to recuperate."

As we rested, a large animal, black and furry with goat-like horns, sauntered across the trail in front of us. *A Himalayan Tahr!* I was excited to see it and took out my special paper to sketch the Tahr. I was glad to see it was still dry.

After we left our rest area, we walked for a few hours and passed many porters, both men and women. They carried large wicker baskets filled with grains, oranges, wood, and other things. Some porters had large sacks balanced on top of their full baskets. Porters carry their heavy baskets close to their backs and hold them in place by a trump line, a strap that wraps around the top of their heads.

Sometimes I heard "*jai dung, dunga, ma . . . yo desimay ro ho*" as porters sang Sherpa folk songs while they trudged up the trail under the weight of their burdens.

Phura Tharkey said, "We've had a tiring day today so we will spend the night in a village close by."

We were in a beautiful little valley with magnificent lofty peaks that towered above us. Brilliant glaciers hung on the edges of the peaks. Their aquamarine blue and white waters flowed down to the glistening *Dudh Kosi* River, the Milk River. As we descended on the rough, rocky trail, we could hear the roar of the river below.

"Wow!" I exclaimed "What a mighty river!

"Yes, due to the storm it's even more powerful than usual because the water level is higher," Phura Tharkey explained. "I hope we can cross it without any difficulties."

I recognized the pastels from my paints. "Why is it aquamarine and white?" I asked.

"This water flows from a glacier," Phura Tharkey explained. "Its blue color is caused by particles of glacial rock which are suspended in the water, and its white color is due to foam that forms as the water rushes over the rocks."

"Interesting. Thank you for that explanation," I replied.

I could see that the area below Namche Bazaar was quite different than the Khumjung area. People grew green leafy vegetables and orange carrots instead of only potatoes. Butterflies hovered over yellow flowers, and on the marble rocks above us bees created hives of honey. Waterfalls cascaded from the high hills down to the deep gorges. Sweet-smelling pines and tall rhododendron trees grew everywhere.

"Can we stop here for a few minutes so I can draw a picture of this gorgeous scenery?" I asked. "I know Mother would love to see it."

"Yes," said Phura Tharkey. "That's a fine idea."

It was nice to sit down and draw for a moment, until Uncle complained. "If you stop to draw pictures all the time, we'll never get to Kathmandu! The king wants us there as soon as possible, and I want to get back to Khumjung sooner than later. We still have a long distance to go to get to Kathmandu."

"Okay but first let me finish this picture," I pleaded.

"If you must, then do it fast," Uncle replied.

It's obvious Uncle doesn't know that it takes time to draw a good picture, I thought.

Reluctantly I packed up my drawing materials, and we continued on our journey. We hiked up ridges and down to deep river gorges, down and up, up and down we went. We made good progress toward Lukla, our day's destination; but then, the ground beneath us shook. It felt like a wave.

"Earthquake!" I screamed, "Let's get under that rock overhang and cover our heads!"

Whoosh!

Boulders and dirt roared past us. Rocks crashed into each other. It sounded like thunder. Sparks flew. Branches broke off trees. The trail in front of us disappeared!

My heart beat as loud as drums in a Buddhist temple. My hair whipped in front of my face. It was hard to catch my breath. I couldn't speak. I felt like I had butterflies in my stomach.

Uncle and I grasped each other and held on. Our legs wobbled, we were so frightened and disoriented. But since the rock protected us, we didn't get hit by falling objects.

I cried out, "We could have been killed. That was so scary!"

"Where is Phura Tharkey? Is he ok? Did he get buried in the landslide?" Uncle answered.

Phura Tharkey soon appeared, but he walked with a limp and his face was scratched.

"What happened?" I asked.

With wide eyes and worried lines on his forehead, Phura Tharkey looked around to make sure we were safe before he sat down and talked with us. "My leg that had polio sometimes gets aggravated and makes me limp. Also, a branch slid down the hill, hit my face, and scratched me. But I'll be all right."

I exclaimed, "This day has been awful! I was almost kidnapped. It rained hard on us. Uncle slid down the muddy hillside. We sloshed through the wet slippery mud, and I fell face first into it. We were shaken by an earthquake, then a landslide almost swept us down the mountain."

I sighed, "If we had stayed home none of this would have happened. I could have taken the school test, and Uncle could have worked on the stone house he has been building. I could have worked for him and earned money to pay for school. Instead, here we are in these horrible conditions. Phura Tharkey, maybe you have the wrong Sonam Sherpa? There are several of us who look similar and have the same name."

Maybe you made up this whole thing I continued in my own mind. Maybe you aren't a messenger from the king. Maybe the king doesn't even exist.

"You don't even know what problem the king wants me to help him solve."

This is stupid. We should go home! I'd rather take care of my sheep than continue on this journey.

Phura Tharkey's voice was compassionate, "It has been a hard day for you, Sonam. I understand why you are upset. Trust me, the king did send me to get you. Remember I showed you the official summons for Sonam Sherpa of Khumjung, signed by the king himself?"

Then more sternly he added "Remember, if you don't respond to the summons there are consequences. For a month, you would have to wear a bright red shirt that indicates you did not respond. You would have to stand up in front of the whole community and explain why you did not respond. You would have to create a protected field where the community can plant potatoes and build four stone walls, one meter high and five meters long, around it."

That sounded awful. "I will continue on this journey, even though it is difficult," I relented.

Phura Tharkey then reassured us, "We are quite close to the bridge, and after we cross it there's a village where we can spend the night. There we'll find a tea house where we can eat something and a stone hut where we can sleep on the veranda. It should only take about one more hour until we arrive."

We trudged on. Soon we came to a flat open area where there were a few stone huts and a few young children played in the field. But the rest of the hamlet seemed to be deserted.

Phura Tharkey pointed. "A short distance beyond this field is the bridge where we'll cross the river,"

Uncle and I scanned the area. We didn't see any bridge. We looked at each other, shrugged our shoulders, and shook our heads. Phura Tharkey walked ahead of us and disappeared behind a huge boulder.

That's when we heard him cry out loudly. *Was that a swear word? From the king's emissary?*

We ran ahead and found Phura Tharkey in despair. "I know we're at the right place on the river. The bridge was here. I saw those stone huts near the bridge when I walked across it a few days ago."

Phura Tharkey sighed, "The bridge must have been destroyed in the storm and earthquake! Look over there on the far side of the river. The piles of stones that held up the bridge on my way to Khujung have fallen down and are scattered on the ground next to some of the bridge's wooden beams."

"Now we'll never get to Kathmandu!" I despaired, "If we can't cross the river, we'll never get to meet the king! There must be a way to cross."

Eight

The bridge to the village where we'd hoped to finally sleep was washed out.

We knew we would never get to Kathmandu if we couldn't find another way to cross. So Uncle, Phura Tharkey, and I searched up and down the riverside, but we could not find one.

Finally, Phura Tharkey said, "I'll go and see if there is anybody in those stone huts. Maybe they can show us a place to cross."

When he returned, he was accompanied by a young woman and a young man. They looked like brother and sister.

With our hands in the prayer position, we greeted each other, "Namaste."

The young woman said, "Phura Tharkey told us about your day. You must be tired and hungry. Please come into our humble home and have some tea and something to eat."

I blurted out, "Yes, it was an *awful* day, and I'm famished!"

Uncle was more gracious. "This is a kind invitation. It would be nice to have some tea, but we can't stay long. We need to be on our way soon."

We followed them to their stone hut, and Uncle noticed a corner of their hut had fallen down. He whispered to me: "I *could* fix that, but I hope they don't ask me to. It could take several days, and I don't want this trip to last any longer than necessary. I do need to get back to Khumjung and work on the house I'm building there."

While we drank tea the young woman asked me, "Tell me about your life in Khumjung."

"My mother weaves yak wool blankets and my father guides climbers up Sagarmatha. I am a shepherd, and I like to draw. I'm also a very good student, and I hope to go to an excellent secondary school, because I'm curious about a lot of things and want to learn more."

The woman was delighted. "I am a teacher at a secondary school in Lukla!"

Excited, I asked, "Please tell me about your school."

"Our school is excellent."

"What do you teach?"

"I teach social studies and science."

"Do you know what the requirements are to attend your school?"

"I'm not sure, but if you'd like to visit the school you can ask the headmaster."

"We are on our way to Kathmandu. Is Lukla on the way?"

"Yes, it is. Many of the older boys from Namche Bazaar attend that school."

"Is the school in session now?"

"Yes, but I took some time off to care for my grandfather who had an injury," the teacher explained. "I hope you are able to attend an excellent school. Education is so important."

"Have you heard of a school in Kathmandu called *Budhanilkantha?*"

"No, I'm not familiar with that one."

It was silent for a moment, then Phura Tharkey told the man and woman, "Mingma is an excellent builder, he builds stone houses."

"Our grandfather, who we live with here, built this hut himself. But a week ago, he had an accident so he can't build any more. In the earthquake, part of our hut fell down."

"Let's go look at the problem," Phura Tharkey said. "Mingma could probably fix that for you."

We walked outside and looked at the part that was destroyed. As the two young people walked ahead of us, Uncle glared at Phura Tharkey and with clenched jaw whispered, "Why did you tell them I build houses. It could take many days to repair, and you said the king wants us to arrive as soon as possible. Maybe we'll miss the appointment with the king if we don't keep moving. Then we will have wasted this whole trip!"

In a whisper, I added, "If we were at home, I could earn money to pay for school, but now we must continue our trek to Kathmandu, for if we don't meet with the king, I'll have to pay the consequences."

The young woman overheard our conversation and inquired, "What do you mean when you say you are on your way to meet the king? What king? Is this a made-up story?"

"No, it is true. The king has summoned me to Kathmandu to see him. Phura Tharkey is his messenger."

"Why did the king summon *you*?" she asked.

"He wants me to help him solve a problem, but none of us knows what it is. It's a mystery. I only know that he summoned me, and I must go." For Uncle's sake I added, "That's why we can't stay here long."

Phura Tharkey spoke now, "That's true, we are eager to be on our way soon. Also, this is my first emissary job, and I want to please King Birendra. He asked me to return as soon as possible with Sonam. "But," he went on, "we also want to give you something for your kind hospitality, and we know it would help you most if Mingma fixes your hut."

"Yes, it would!" the young woman replied.

I asked the young man, "Do you know how we can cross the river?"

"Yes, I can tell you how to cross the river. But first will you help us fix our hut?"

To Phura Tharkey and Uncle, I whispered, "It seems to me that we can either stay and fix the hut, or we could go and explore some more on our own and try to find a place to cross. If we find another way we can leave sooner. How about if Uncle looks at the problem and figures out what needs to be done and Phura Tharkey and I continue to search for another crossing?"

The young man overheard me and offered, "Our grandfather told us that down river there are some boulders that you can use to cross, but between here and there is a waterfall that you have to traverse. It will not be easy, but you should be able to cross the river there."

Then the young woman said, "I have an idea. It would be easier for you to cross the river in the morning. You can stay here tonight, and Mingma can assess the problem and teach my brother how to fix it. In the morning, when you have more energy, we'll lead you to the river to make sure you get to the right location."

Uncle said, "This sounds like a good idea!" and we all agreed. We were exhausted and dirty from the mud and the landslide.

Uncle and the young man studied the corner of the hut. It was quite an extensive problem that would take the young man many days to repair. Uncle explained the repair to me along with the young man, and we all worked together until it got dark, in the early evening. Uncle reassured the young man that he would stop by on his way back to Khumjung to check on the repair and offer his help if needed.

Uncle told me "The things you learn here will be of value when you help me with Sir Edmund Hillary's house in Khumjung. When we work on that, I will pay you money that you can use to pay for school." That sounded good to me.

That night, before I fell asleep, I thought about the king and the palace.

I hope I make it to the palace. I hope I don't fall down anymore and we don't have any more delays. I wonder what the king looks like? What problem does he want me, a peasant boy, to help him, a king, solve? Am I supposed to talk to the King! What should I say?

The next morning was sunny, and the sky was brilliant blue. We felt refreshed after a good night's sleep and expected it would be a good day. With the young woman and the young man, we climbed a steep hillside and scaled a rock wall to get above the waterfall they'd mentioned. It was a strenuous climb!

At the top we crossed a small river, then descended the bank next to the waterfall, being careful to not disrupt the rocks at the edge of the falls. We arrived at the place where the young man had indicated we could cross the river. It was wider and not as deep as in the gorge, but due to the increased amount of water from the storm, the current was swift! It swirled around hut sized boulders.

If we could climb on top of the boulders and if we were careful, it looked like we could make it across.

Phura Tharkey went first and crossed on the boulders.

Uncle and I tried to follow him. Uncle made it across without any difficulties, but being shorter my legs didn't reach as far. I slipped, and the turbulent water grabbed me!

The current twisted my body and pulled me down! I thought I would drown!

Then one surge of the river pushed me up, and I gasped for air! "Help!" I yelped.

I tried to grab ahold of the boulder, but all I could do was claw at the air. I was pushed down again, and my foot scraped against the rock. My shoe came off and careened down the river.

Phura Tharkey ran back. He and Uncle pulled me out of the river, shivering and shaking.

"Brrr, that river water is so cold!!" I crossed my arms and held them close to my chest.

Uncle wrapped his strong arms around me. They warmed and comforted me.

"At least I don't look like a muddy Yeti like I did yesterday," I laughed, relieved, and then we all laughed.

Phura Tharkey pondered. "It'll be safer for me to carry you. Climb onto my back."

"*Thuche*, Phura Tharkey, you are so kind to me!"

Despite his limp, he was sure-footed as we crossed the raging river, and I was relieved to be on solid ground again.

Phura Tharkey built a fire to warm me and dry out my clothes, and he made some hot chai.

"How can I get to Kathmandu with only one shoe? I can't hop on one foot. I can't meet the king barefoot," I muttered. "We have to return to Namche Bazaar to buy some shoes."

Uncle replied, "There's not enough time to go back. We must go on to Lukla then Kathmandu. I'll make you a shoe out of grasses—or you can go barefoot like some of the porters do. We'll buy shoes for you in Kathmandu."

While he wove the grasses together into a shoe, I thought of all the pictures I had drawn on our trip. "Oh no!" I cried, "My pictures must be ruined! Mother will be so disappointed."

I rummaged through my soggy bag to find the pictures. Much to my surprise, the copper box had kept my pictures dry. I was so lucky. *Ganesh must have helped me!*

After Uncle finished the shoe, I put it on my foot. It was not comfortable, but it would be better than nothing.

We continued our journey to Kathmandu. When we passed people on the well-marked trail, we all said "Namaste." We passed, always on our right side, big mani rocks with *Om mani padme hum* carved on them. As we passed, we chanted the powerful yet pure Buddhist mantra, "*Om mani padme hum.*" Prayer flags fluttered in the gentle breeze. We had a feeling that life was good, and our hardships were behind us.

Phura Tharkey told us, "We'll go to Lukla because there is an airfield there where we can take a flight to Kathmandu."

As we walked towards Lukla, Uncle Mingma told us about the creation of the airfield. "I heard about the Lukla airfield from many Sherpa friends who told me stories about how this 'most dangerous airfield in the world' was built. Sir Edmund Hillary designed it and taught them how to build it. He was concerned about the soil resistance. He wondered if the soil at that site could hold an airplane. *Could they make the field flat enough for a plane to land?* To solve these problems, he got hundreds of Sherpas to link arms and sing and dance for several days, a foot-stomping, 16-step dance to flatten down the barren earth on the edge of the steep cliff! The Sherpas worked with dignity, courage, and much good humor in spite of their fear that they could fall off the cliff and die. I never dreamed that one day I would stand, with my nephew, on this airfield about to take a flight from it!"

When we arrived in the village of Lukla, Phura Tharkey said, "Our flight should leave in about an hour. I'll go to the airport to check on it."

When he returned, he said, "Our flight has been delayed till tomorrow. Pilots can fly safely only when the skies are clear, and this afternoon there are too many clouds in Kathmandu. We'll stay in Lukla tonight." Phura Tharkey bemoaned the situation, "The king allowed for us to take three days from Khumjung to Kathmandu, but we have taken more than that. He'll probably be angry with me. He might not let me continue to be his emissary. He may not have time to meet with us."

Uncle replied, "We are doing the best we can. We can hope the king understands and will still be able to meet with us."

I said, "Since we have more time in Lukla, can we visit the secondary school the kind young woman in the stone hut told us about? She told me I could ask the headmaster some questions about the requirements to attend school there. It's where the boys from Namche Bazaar go to school."

"Yes, that is a good idea," replied Phura Tharkey brightening.

We found our way to the school. I was excited. *Maybe this is where I'll go to secondary school!*

I ran up to the door with high hopes of meeting the headmaster, but instead I found a note tacked to the door:

SCHOOL CLOSED UNTIL FURTHER NOTICE DUE TO DAMAGE CAUSED BY THE EARTHQUAKE. IN EMERGENCY, CONTACT THE HEADMASTER, HAJUR TASHI SHERPA.

In despair mixed with hope I said, "Let's try to find where the headmaster lives and talk with him at his house."

"If it is really important to you, we can try to do that," Phura Tharkey replied. "Since Lukla is small, we can probably find someone who knows the headmaster."

As we left the school building, I saw a boy about my age. I wondered if he was a student at the school. He had a backpack with the name of the school on it. I wondered, *Was he a bully or a kind boy?*

I shyly approached him. "Excuse me, do you know where the headmaster lives?"

"Yes," he replied with hesitancy.

"Can you show me the way to his house?"

"Why do you want to go there?"

"The school door was locked, and it said if there's an emergency to contact the headmaster."

"What is the emergency?" the boy asked.

"It's not really an emergency, but I want to find out about the requirements to attend the school. I heard it's an excellent school. I am from Khumjung, and I have to leave Lukla for Kathmandu tomorrow, so I don't have time to wait for the school to re-open."

"Okay, I'll take you to his house. What is your name?"

"My name is Sonam Sherpa. What is yours?"

"I am Norbu Sherpa."

"Do you go to the school?"

"Yes."

"Can you please tell me about the classes you take?"

"We have excellent teachers and classes."

"What's your favorite subject?"

"Math is my favorite subject."

"My papa thinks I should become a businessman, but I don't want to. I'm not interested in math. With your interest in math, Norbu, you could become a businessman. My favorite subject is science. When I was on my way here, I met your school's social studies and science teacher. Please tell me about your science class."

"I think it's disgusting. We have to cut up frogs and rats and look inside of them."

"I think that would be fascinating."

Norbu said, "The part of science I do like is learning about plants and animals that live near us. I also like astronomy class where we study the stars. It's fun to make up stories to describe the star patterns, the constellations. In music we learn Nepali folk songs, and in our art class we learn to draw."

"I like to draw too. I've drawn pictures of many things we've seen along the way from Khumjung to here. Your classes sound so interesting! I think I would like to attend your school. I need to talk with the headmaster to see if I can. I hope he is home."

Norbu took us to the headmaster's house. I felt nervous to knock on the door. I must have looked so weird wearing the grass shoe. But then I remembered Papa's advice. *If I don't take a risk, nothing will change.*

The headmaster saw us outside and opened his door. He looked happy to see Norbu. Then he introduced himself to us, "I am Hajur Tashi Sherpa. What can I do for you?"

Phura Tharkey replied, "Namaste, Hajur Sherpa. I am Phura Tharkey from Kathmandu, and this is my young friend, Sonam Sherpa from Khumjung. We would like to find out about your school. Sonam, tell Hajur Sherpa what you want."

"Namaste, Hajur Sherpa. I am Sonam Sherpa, and I live in Khumjung. I tried to visit your school, but it was closed. There was a note on the door that said that in an emergency to contact the headmaster. Though it's not a true emergency, we are on our way to Kathmandu and must leave Lukla in the morning. Norbu showed us the way to your home. I am sorry to bother you at home."

"Come in."

The kind headmaster served us tea then asked, "How can I help you?"

"I want to attend an excellent secondary school. We met the woman who teaches social studies and science, and she told me about your school. Then we met Norbu, and he told us about some of the classes. I am a top student in the highest grade at my school in Khumjung. I would like to learn what the requirements are to attend the Lukla school. Please tell me about your school and the admission requirements."

He told us much about the school, but sadly he added, "I am sorry to have to tell you this, but at the present time there are no spaces available in our school. We are full for the next two years. I can put you on a wait list if you wish."

Disappointed, I said. "Yes, please do add my name to the wait list. And thank you for taking time to talk with us!"

Another thwarted opportunity! I couldn't take the entrance exam in Khumjung, I didn't have enough money to pay for school, and this school was full! I was so frustrated.

Am I destined to be a shepherd for the rest of my life? Then why am I curious about so many things I can't learn except by going to school?

Uncle didn't help any when he said, "I don't know why you are so determined to get more education. I only went to third grade, and I am well employed and have a good life."

"That's not enough for me. I am thirsty to learn. Just look at the things we've learned in the past few days! And soon, we will learn about flight when we take a plane ride! Imagine how much more there is to learn in life beyond that! It's exciting to learn. Come on Uncle, let's go explore Lukla and see what we can learn here."

That night, we stayed at a tea house in Lukla, and early the next morning we went to the airfield. Phura Tharkey said, "We need to buy our tickets and show the airline agent our papers. Our plane to Kathmandu should arrive in about an hour."

We were awestruck as we stood on 'the most dangerous airfield of the world'!

"Uncle, look at that runway! It goes so steeply downhill that if a pilot makes a mistake the plane would crash into the deep river gorge below us! If it doesn't crash, the pilot would have to get the plane to rise to clear the top of the mountain on the other side of the gorge!" I pointed up in the sky to the top of the mountain.

Exciting as it was to learn, still the thought of flying made me shake. Beads of sweat formed on my forehead, and Uncle remarked that my face looked pale. I saw that he too was nervous.

"I'm really afraid to leave the earth in a plane that's made of a thin sheet of metal," I admitted. "Birds fly, but I'm not a bird!"

Uncle nodded in agreement. Neither of us ever thought we'd go up in the sky and fly with the birds. That seemed outrageous! Even though I was scared, a part of me was curious to see how it would feel to be in an airplane and to fly with the Bar-Headed Geese and Rosy Minivets.

Phura Tharkey saw how dumbfounded we were and tried to alleviate our anxiety. He pointed out, "There have been hundreds of flights out of Lukla without any problems. Sonam, there's enough time for you to draw a picture of the airfield so you can show your mother and others in Khumjung what it looks like."

Maybe he's just trying to calm my fears, I thought, but I liked the idea. I sat down, got out my special paper and pastels, and drew a picture.

After a while, we heard a rumble as the plane approached. *Oh no, oh yes, oh no, here it is!* A litany that soared through my brain. Then I looked over and saw on the edge of the airfield a plane that had crashed!

That could happen to us.

Now I was really afraid. Uncle Mingma was fearful too and resisted getting on the plane.

He has to get on the plane! If we don't, we'll never get to Kathmandu to meet the king.

Nine

Seeing our fear, Phura Tharkey spoke with Uncle and me for a long time. "Although the airfield is dangerous," he admitted "all the pilots who fly here have good safety records."

As he spoke, we watched several planes land. Each time, the airport crew efficiently unloaded cargo, loaded new luggage, and helped the passengers board. Then we watched the planes take off again. The whole thing was like a well-choreographed dance.

Finally, Uncle became convinced that it would be all right to fly, so we boarded the plane. Uncle held onto the handrail and

climbed the stairs, one slow step at a time. The flight attendant showed him where to sit.

I followed him and found a seat next to a window. Uncle shut his eyes, hid his head, and prayed. My stomach felt like it had butterflies inside it, but I was curious, so I looked out the window and held my breath.

The Twin Otter plane, with nineteen passengers on board, roared downhill on the grassy runway. It seemed like it would fall into the abyss below! Then, it choked and sputtered.

Uncle trembled and with sweaty hands grabbed his chest.

I gasped, held on tight to the seat, and exclaimed, "We're gonna crash!"

At the last minute, the plane lifted off the earth then flew high above the ridges. We flew with the birds above the steep mountains and deep valleys on our way to Kathmandu!

I relaxed and became so enthralled by the adventure I couldn't sit still in my seat. I watched the instruments on the pilot's dashboard change as the altitude and directions changed. Out my window I saw beautiful scenery—the jagged snowy summits and brown foothills of the Himalayas, and green farms along the Bagmati River.

As we approached the gigantic city of Kathmandu, I could see Tribhuvan International airport. All too soon the flight was over. The pilot brought us down from the sky and landed the plane on the flat tarmac runway without any problems.

Flying is so exciting, I thought. When I get my education, it would be fun to become a pilot.

Phura Tharkey told us, "Before we left Lukla, I contacted the palace staff and told them when we would arrive so there should be someone here to meet us. We'll walk through the airport and outside to the far side of the building. The chauffeur should be there in a big black car. He'll drive us to the guest house where you will stay."

I had never seen a real car before, let alone ridden in one. I was eager to see it.

It was a huge black car, like a big cave—big enough to fit three sheep and some chickens inside. I had only seen such a big car in a picture in my schoolbooks.

I crawled into the backseat beside Uncle, and Phura Tharkey rode beside the king's chauffeur in the front seat. It felt strange to be inside a fancy car instead of outside on the roadside with the masses of people. I felt like a prince!

It took us a long time to drive from the Kathmandu airport to the guest house near the king's palace, the Narayanhiti Palace. As we rode through the city, we saw tall, unusually shaped buildings with five tiers of roofs stacked on top of each other like a stack of pancakes. I saw a frightening sculpture. It had a black stone face and wore a huge necklace and a headdress of skulls. It had six arms two of which carried weapons, and stood on top of a demon, crushing its body.

"He is Kaal Bhairav, the Hindu god of time and destruction—but also of re-creation," Phura Tharkey informed us.

I got shivers up my spine. "I hope he doesn't destroy us!"

After a while, we parked at a narrow, curving path. "This path leads to the place where we'll stay" Phura Tharkey told us.

We walked down the path and came to a house. Phura Tharkey opened the door and invited us inside.

"Look," Uncle said, "There's no smoke in the kitchen! The air is so clean. How is that possible?"

Phura Tharkey replied, "The kitchen has an electric stove. It doesn't burn wood so there's no smoke."

"That's nice!"

"Where will we sleep?" I asked. "There are no sleeping pads on the floor."

Phura Tharkey explained "You can sleep on these beds that are raised off the floor, and you can sit on these soft comfortable chairs."

"How luxurious! Do we go outside to use the bathroom?" Uncle asked.

"No, I'll show you the bathroom here inside."

Phura Tharkey opened the door to a small room and inside was a toilet that a person would sit on—instead of a floor toilet that we squat to use. *How unusual!* The guest house was nice, but so different than home.

More important than the guest house was that the next day I, an eleven-year-old peasant boy from Khumjung, was going to meet the king of Nepal! That was beyond belief.

Again, I wondered why I was here.

That night I tossed and turned as I tried to sleep. I felt anxious yet excited. Finally, I got to sleep, then, what seemed like moments later, the dawn light appeared.

On this most special day of my life, I jumped out of bed, deciding to explore the place. I walked down a hallway, turned a corner and then ran right into a servant girl.

Oops!

The tray wobbled in her hands, but fortunately she didn't drop it. "I have some bed tea for you," she muttered.

"I'm sorry I ran into you! I didn't think anyone else was awake."

It was a comfort to have a cup of tea, but Grandma's Tibetan chai tasted better. Uncle and Phura Tharkey got up and had some tea too.

My gurgling stomach was hungry so I was glad when the servant brought breakfast. It looked tasty, but different than what I was used to.

She explained what we would eat. "Here are some fried eggs and chapatis, and these fruits are pineapple, papaya, and mango."

I was pleased to see the same unusual fruits I had drawn in Namche Bazaar. Now I would find out what they tasted like! The pineapple was sweet and also a little acidic; the papaya and mangos were sweet and smooth. They were all delicious.

During breakfast, Phura Tharkey described the plan for this monumental day and what we should expect when we visited the king. To our surprise, one of the servants entered the room and said he needed to speak to Phura Tharkey, who excused himself and left the room.

When he returned, he had a look of disappointment on his face. "The appointment with the king will have to wait. The king has official business to conduct today. He had planned to meet with us two days ago, since we planned for only three days to go from Khumjung to Kathmandu. But we took five days due to the kidnapping, the storm, the stone-hut repair, and the river accident." He looked dejected, "I failed the king, and now he won't see us today. I hope I don't lose my emissary job."

Uncle replied, "You told us the king is a fair man who wants to understand his people. It's not your fault that we encountered all those obstacles. In spite of them, you have done a good job getting us to Kathmandu safely. I can't imagine the king will punish you for things you could not control."

Phura Tharkey looked relieved. "I do hope the king will be able to see us sometime soon. But we will have to wait until he can make time in his full schedule."

I was less patient and levelheaded. "Oh nooo! We can't see the king after all!"

Maybe the king never really wanted to see me.

I felt crestfallen, deflated like a balloon that had lost its air. "This whole difficult trip was worth nothing!" I wanted to cry.

Uncle Mingma worried. "Perhaps I shouldn't have volunteered to come on this trip. It will be difficult to get Sir Hillary's house built before his next visit if we have to wait a long time."

"I'm sorry it is this way," Phura Tharkey apologized. But he reminded us, "If you didn't come to meet with the king when he issued a summons, the consequences would have been very strong. While we wait, we can explore many fascinating sites in Kathmandu."

It would be a treat to see famous sites. I brightened at the thought and became so excited that I danced around. I had seen pictures of Durbar Square and Swayambhunath and the king's palace in my school books, but I never thought I'd be able to see them in person!

"Phura Tharkey, you are so nice to us."

When I thought about the pictures in my schoolbooks, it reminded me about the Budhanilkantha School. *It'd be wonderful to visit it while I'm here! I'll ask if we can. While I'm visiting the school maybe I could even take the test that I couldn't take in Khumjung, since we had to leave a day before it was to be administered.*

"Phura Tharkey, I would like to visit the Budhanilkantha School because I would like to go to school there. Can we visit it while we tour Kathmandu today?"

"I wish we could, but they have a school holiday today so no one will be there. Also, it is far from the other places we'll visit."

I felt sad and disappointed. I hadn't been able to take the test in Khumjung or visit the school in Lukla, and now I couldn't even *see* the school in Kathmandu. *Maybe I'm not meant to go to school, and I should stop hoping for that anymore.* Much as I loved and missed my sheep, I knew that if I had to be a shepherd the rest of my life I wouldn't be pleased.

Phura Tharkey told me, "Since you are excited to see the city up close, we can hire a rickshaw cyclist to take us around."

I imagine the king never gets to ride in *rickshaws*. It would be too dangerous for him.

Phura Tharkey went out to the street and arranged for a rickshaw to come to the guest house. The driver was a strong, lean man. Ours was one of many rickshaws on the narrow streets that day.

Phura Tharkey told the driver "Mingma and Sonam are from Khumjung. They have never been to Kathmandu before, so they are delighted to have the opportunity to see the city. But first, we must go to a shop to buy Sonam some new shoes and some nice clothes."

"I am pleased to take them wherever you want me to," the driver said.

Uncle and I climbed onto the seat in one rickshaw, and Phura Tharkey followed us in another one.

As I watched the rickshaw driver, I got a crazy idea. *I'll ask him if I can ride his bicycle.* I imagined he wouldn't let me, since I'm from Khumjung and he'd probably guess that I'd never ridden a bicycle. He'd figure that I'd not last long because it takes a lot of effort to pull two people in a rickshaw. I was sure he wouldn't let me but timidly asked, "Excuse me, Driver. Would it be okay with you if I rode your bicycle and tried to pull the rickshaw for a short distance?"

Much to my surprise, he agreed to let me try. He didn't even ask if I knew how to ride a bike! I got on the bicycle. I almost fell off at first, but soon I figured out how to ride. Since I'm strong, because I tend my sheep in the mountains, I picked up speed and felt confident.

I looked around as I rode, and everything went well until I ran into a pothole in the road and *kerplunk!* The rickshaw toppled over and hit a building, and Uncle and the driver both tumbled out. *Oh NO!*

I was fortunate that no one was hurt and nothing bad had happened to the rickshaw. We picked ourselves up, and the driver righted the rickshaw. But his expression showed he wondered why on earth he'd let me try.

Needless to say, that was the end of my bicycle ride for the day!

When we got resettled, I looked up at the building we had run into. It was one of those tall, unusually shaped wooden, buildings like we had seen from the car coming from the airport. It had five levels of roofs, but no entrance to the inside. *What a strange sight!*

Phura Tharkey explained, "This is a Buddhist temple called a *pagoda*. There are Hindu pagodas as well. The shape symbolizes a sacred mountain."

"The mountains near Khumjung don't look like that," I replied.

The rickshaw driver got back on his bicycle and drove us to a famous centuries-old, three-storied, brick and wooden palace called Kumari Bahal. Its wooden windows were carved into intricate shapes of flowers, mythical beasts, goddesses, and birds. They were carved by *Newar* artists who have lived in this area for two thousand years. The most exquisite one was in the shape of a peacock. It was magnificent!

When I told Phura Tharkey, "I want to draw a picture of the peacock window" he helped me find a place to sit and draw.

As I drew, I heard something that sounded like a crying baby, but looking around I didn't see a baby. Then I heard it again.

It was a peacock in the courtyard. It stood with its iridescent green and blue tail feathers spread out in full glory. It was gorgeous! It was hard to find the exact colors to draw it.

Now, THIS is my most favorite bird, I decided—more than my other favorites, the Rosy Minivet, the Bar-Headed Goose, and the colorful Himalayan Monal Pheasant.

As I drew the peacock many people walked past me and entered the courtyard.

Uncle and I were curious to know why, so we followed them. The people waited and watched.

I asked the man next to me, "What is everyone waiting for?"

He said, "Soon the *Kumari* will appear and bless us."

"What is a Kumari?" I asked.

"She is the living goddess. We all hold her in high esteem."

The people watched in silence as the living goddess made her appearance in the window on the third floor. She wore a lot of ritualistic make up: bright red lipstick, black mascara that extended out to the sides of her face, and red makeup painted in an intricate design on her forehead.

Everyone in the courtyard bowed and greeted her, "Namaste," they said. She blessed us then disappeared after only a couple of minutes.

I looked at Uncle with a look of consternation and said, "She looks like a doll with all those colors on her face. She never smiled. She didn't say anything. I wonder what her life is like?"

Phura Tharkey overheard and explained, "The revered Kumari lives an isolated life inside the palace. Her feet never touch the ground. She leaves the palace only once a year for Kathmandu's biggest festival of the year, Indra Jatra, an eight-day Hindu festival in September that honors her. She dresses in a gold and red dress and wears rings, bracelets, necklaces, a jeweled tiara, and a garland of marigolds. She sits on a golden throne on a chariot that men carry through the streets of Kathmandu. Hundreds of people gather around her and try to touch her feet because it's believed that if we touch her feet she will bring us good fortune, heal our illnesses, and relieve us of our troubles. Once a year, the king visits her in the palace and bows down and kisses her feet."

"How did she become the goddess?" I inquired curiously.

"When she was only four years old, this Newari girl was chosen through a strict, ancient, selection process that identifies her as the living embodiment of the most revered Hindu mother goddess, Durga. Now she is eleven years old, but when she reaches puberty she will return to normal life, and a new kumari will be chosen."

"She's the same age I am! I'm glad I don't have to live a life like that. I'd miss roaming through the hills with my sheep." I wondered if my sheep missed me and if they were all right without me. "Life in Khumjung is very different than in the big city of Kathmandu."

Phura Tharkey commented, "Yes that's true. Here we have many festivals—more Newari festivals than there are days of the year!"

boom! Boom! **BOOM!**

Our conversation was interrupted by drumbeats, each one louder as a parade approached us. Musicians played loud music on drums, brass, trumpet-like instruments, cymbals, and long Tibetan horns. Masked demon dancers with ferocious faces and protruding fangs jumped and kicked and danced with wild movements.

Big colorful floats appeared, and a crowd of people followed the parade. The energy was contagious so we joined them.

We walked down narrow alleys into Durbar Square. We gazed at numerous pagoda style temples with detailed carvings, dedicated to Hindu gods. Phura Tharkey explained, "That temple is dedicated to Shiva, the supreme lord of Hindus, with its statue of the lord's vehicle, a bronze bull, outside." I was tempted to climb up to sit on it, but I didn't.

Another temple was dedicated to Vishnu, the protector of the order of things. In front of that temple was the mythical eagle bird, Garuda. Since I love birds, I sometimes like to pretend that I am Garuda.

Out of the drum temple came a deep booming sound as a Hindu priest beat a gigantic drum. I noticed that the drum was wider than I was tall.

My favorite temple was the one dedicated to the elephant-headed Ganesh. He is the remover of obstacles, bringer of good luck, supporter of arts, sciences, intellect, and wisdom. It pleased me to see that temple because Ganesh has treated me so well.

As we passed another building, I asked, "What is that red statue at the golden doorway that's adorned with snakes, dragons, and a ten-armed goddess?"

Phura Tharkey explained, "The famous, ancient, Hanuman Dhoka palace. Legend tells us that the red-colored monkey god, Hanuman, is strong and loyal and performs daring feats to protect all the kings who are crowned in this palace, which includes King Birendra. Later I'll tell you about his coronation."

That made me think about the king and once again wonder, *Why would such an important person want to meet me, a young, simple peasant boy? What do I have that he needs?*

After our procession through Durbar Square, our rickshaw driver picked us up again and took us to a *stupa* on top of a high hill. "Swayambhunath is known as the monkey temple," and even as Phura Tharkey was telling us this, a little monkey darted out in front of us.

The little monkey scurried up the tree next to the stairs and jumped from tree to tree. I'd never seen a monkey before. "Let's stop and watch that cute monkey."

But Phura Tharkey said, "We'll see lots of holy monkeys at the top of the hill."

That inspired me to run up the long flight of stairs. I counted them as I ran—365 stairs altogether! Along the stairs people sold marigold garlands and candles. The worshippers turned prayer wheels, admired the Hindu monuments, and paid respect to the big golden Buddhas.

Phura Tharkey told us "This is the oldest religious site in all of Nepal, a place where Hindus and Buddhists come together and worship in harmony."

At the top of the hill were Hindu and Buddhist temples and a huge stupa that had the same shape as the one in Khumjung but bigger and more elaborate. Phura Tharkey explained to Uncle and me that stupas represent the enlightened mind of Buddha:

The whitewashed dome represents the earth or the spotless pure jewel of Nirvana.

The nose, that looks like a question mark, represents the unity of all things.

Two eyes look out from each of the four sides of the stupa located above the dome. They are the eyes of the Buddha who sees everywhere, including the panoramic view of the whole Kathmandu valley.

The gilded spire with its thirteen golden disks represents the thirteen steps to complete enlightenment.

And at the top of the stupa was a lotus shaped parasol with a crescent and a sun disk, topped with a gem representing enlightenment.

Prayer wheels surround the whole stupa. "People walk clockwise with the wheels on their right. They turn each wheel as they chant, *om mani padme hum,*" Phura Tharkey concluded.

It was interesting to learn about the stupa, but I felt like its eyes stared at me wherever I went. I decided to draw a picture of it to show Mother. I sat down near the stupa and opened my copper box to take out my special paper and pastels.

When I opened the box, a monkey, much bigger than the cute little one from before, jumped up and grabbed the shiny copper lid of my box!

Oh No! I froze in disbelief.

Then I remembered the two stones I aways carried in my pocket. Grabbing one, I tried to hit the monkey, but he moved too fast, and I missed!

I ran after the monkey to get the lid back. "Stop! Give me my lid!"

A whole troop of monkeys scampered over to see what the commotion was about. Mature ones jumped up on shrines, babies rode on their mother's backs, young monkeys picked salt off each other's sweaty bodies, and more curious monkeys pawed through my papers!

These monkeys' screeching was obnoxious and overwhelming.

Luckily, Uncle and Phura Tharkey were able to scare the monkeys away and save my special papers and the drawings I had made along our trip!

"But that monkey stole the lid to my copper box!" I exclaimed. "He carried it up to the top of the metal roof that covers the prayer wheels, then ran along the roof and jumped over the peak where he dropped it, and now my lid's stuck on the far side of the roof! How can I get it back?"

The roof above the prayer wheels was too high for anyone to reach over the top to retrieve the lid, but I came up with an elaborate plan: I could sneak to the back of the prayer wheels, climb up on the back of the lion statue and up the rack, then hold onto the strut as I banged on the roof. Then the lid should slide down, and I could jump down to the back of the prayer wheels and pick it up!

As I climbed up, I heard a shrill whistle. I looked over and saw a security guard with a stern look on his face. "Hey. Kid! Get down! This is a sacred site not a place to climb!" he yelled at me.

I shouted back, "Sir, that monkey stole the lid to my important copper box. He has it on the other side on the roof above the prayer wheels!"

"Likely story! Come down!" the guard ordered, "and if I see you up there again, I'll take you to the police station."

Ten

The monkey stared at me victoriously from the top of the roof over the prayer wheels.

I have your lid! He seemed to mock me. *Too bad you can't get it!* His attitude irritated me.

I prayed, *Ganesh, you know how to overcome obstacles. Please, help me get my lid.*

I tried to explain to the guard, "I need to get my lid before we leave here to go see the king."

"What king?" he inquired in disbelief.

"King Birendra Bir Bikram Shah Dev."

"Don't tell me lies! How would you, peasant boy, get an audience with the king?"

"It's true. The king summoned me, so I must go to see him. His messenger Phura Tharkey delivered the summons to me. Will you please help me get the lid?"

Hearing his name and how upset I was, Phura Tharkey came over to find out how he could help defuse the problem.

"This young boy lied to me and seems to have delusions of grandeur," the security guard told him. "He thinks he has a visit with the king of Nepal!"

Respectfully, Phura Tharkey responded. "Yes Sir, but the boy is correct, and before we can leave here to go meet the king, we must get his copper lid back."

Uncle brought the copper box over and showed the guard that the lid was gone.

Disbelief on his face and sarcasm in his voice, the guard said, "I hope you have a good visit with the king and are able to get your lid back." Then he walked away.

I shook my head. "He still doesn't believe that we are invited to have an audience with the king, and he didn't help us at all!"

But Uncle said, "Let's get that lid and get out of here before he arrests us. I saw a branch under the trees we passed on our way up the hill. I'll get it and sweep the lid off the roof then, Sonam, you can sneak behind the prayer wheels and pick it up. Phura Tharkey, can you keep a lookout for the guard?"

Thank goodness the plan worked, and we put the waterproof copper box back together. We climbed down the 365 stairs to where the rickshaw driver waited to drive us back to the guest house.

When we got there the servant spoke with Phura Tharkey. "The king rearranged his full schedule, and tomorrow he will have the audience with you."

Phew, thank goodness, I thought. It's not a wasted trip after all. Instead it's better than we imagined it would be. Today we got to explore many fascinating sights in Kathmandu, and tomorrow we get to meet the king!

The next day I woke up early in the morning. *THIS IS THE BIG DAY! THE DAY I WILL MEET THE KING OF NEPAL! Me, little Sonam, from little village Khumjung. I can't believe it!* I had to pinch myself to believe it was all true.

Over breakfast, Phura Tharkey gave us the plan for the day. "At nine o'clock, the king's chauffeur will pick us up here at the guest house and drive us to the Narayanhiti Palace. The king's servants will meet us there and show us around the palace grounds. Then they will take us to the waiting room where they will coach you, Sonam, on how to have an audience with the king. When they deem you are ready, they will show us to the throne room where you will meet King Birendra."

When I heard all these plans, I felt nervous and scared. I asked Phura Tharkey, "What am I supposed to do when I see the king? What should I say?"

In a calm voice, Phura Tharkey reassured me, "The servants will prepare you for the visit once you are inside the palace. Go now and get ready. Put on your best clothes, then meet me in the entrance area of the guest house at 8:45 sharp!"

I was so nervous it was hard to get dressed. I put my pants on backward, my sweater on inside out, and I nearly put my new shoes on the wrong feet! Finally I got everything right after I remembered what Mother had told me: "If you are nervous, sit down and take five deep breaths. Breathe in and out, in and out . . . " That made me feel calmer. I was ready to go for the biggest adventure of my life.

Soon the chauffeur arrived and drove us in the big black car to the Narayanhiti Palace. We entered through massive iron gates and drove to the main entrance of the palace. On both sides of the front door, Gurkha guards stood at attention tall, straight and still. They each held a sharp *kukri* knife and a bayonet.

I would not want to get on the wrong side of them!

A servant girl met us at the door and guided us around the palace grounds. As we walked, I looked up into the tall trees and saw large, black, ugly, creatures that hung upside down. I was afraid to walk under them because I'd never seen them before. *They might fall on me!* But our guide, sensing my fear, said, "Don't be afraid. They're just fruit bats; they like to eat the fruit in those trees."

Phura Tharkey pointed out where the staff quarters were, and his own home. As we looked, we were startled by a loud *grooowllll*. Both Uncle Mingma and I jumped.

Off to the side of the walkway, tucked under a tree, was a large cage with two orange and black Bengal tigers in it! "I hope the cage is strong enough to hold the tigers! Could they escape and attack us?"

Phura Tharkey assured us, "I'm sure you will be safe. You might be interested to know that tigers and elephants come from the Terai region in the south of Nepal. The king likes them; that is why they are here."

"Terai is the home place of the nice vendor in Namche Bazaar whose fruit I liked to draw. So many fascinating things come from the Terai!" I said.

Through the leaves of the trees, I caught a glimpse of a large grey animal walking towards us. Even though it was very big, it walked quietly so I hadn't fully seen nor heard it until it got quite close. Then I saw it was a huge elephant!

"This is Prem Prasad," Phura Tharkey introduced us, "He is the very elephant that the king and queen rode together after their coronation."

My interest piqued, I asked, "Would this be a good time for you to tell us the story of their coronation?"

"Yes, let's sit down by this beautiful pond where koi swim and play in the waters and pink lotus flowers grow." When we were seated, he spoke. "Now I'll tell you the story . . . "

"Remember the Hanuman Dhoka Palace, where we saw Hanuman, the red, monkey-god that guarded the entrance? That's where the ceremony took place. At the auspicious hour of 8:37 on Monday morning February 24th, the ceremony commenced. It was quite elaborate! First, the priests performed a ritual bathing ceremony. They smeared King Birendra's body with mud, taken from several symbolic places—the bottom of a lake, a mountain top, the confluence of two rivers, the doorstep of a special person's house, and the tusk of an elephant." Phura Tharkey explained that this symbolized the King's awareness of the land and his closeness to the people.

"Getting smeared with mud sounds awful, yet, sort of fun," I said.

"After he got smeared with mud, he was cleansed with butter, milk, yogurt, and honey, while priests chanted praises and salutations. Then, they placed an exquisite crown on his head. It was emerald-green encrusted with shimmering jewels: diamonds, pearls, emeralds, and rubies, and adorned with long white feathers from a gorgeous bird of paradise. On the head of his wife, Queen Aishwarya, the chief priest placed the glittering, Nepalese diamond tiara."

"Wow! That sounds wonderful! I wish I could have seen them. I hope he will wear his crown when we meet the king. Will he?" I inquired.

Phura Tharkey considered. "Maybe he will wear it, although that would be unusual."

"After the coronation," he continued, "the king and queen climbed up a ladder and sat on a gilded throne atop of their favorite elephant, Prem Prasad, who was decorated with a jeweled forehead covering and a scarlet and golden tapestry. There were twenty-two other big elephants, each dressed in a red blanket that covered their sides and forehead. Together all the elephants paraded through the streets of Kathmandu. Hundreds of people jostled to catch a glimpse of the king and queen as they rode from Hanuman Dhoka Palace to Narayanhiti Palace! With Prem Prasad on the palace grounds, King Birendra is reminded of his coronation and his promise to serve the people who live throughout the kingdom of Nepal."

"Thank you, Phura Tharkey, that was a very interesting story." I hoped I would have time to draw pictures of Prem Prasad and all the other animals and the guards, but today I had a more important thing to do—meet the King of Nepal!

After we toured the grounds, we were ushered into the palace by kind servants. To keep us cool in the heat of the day, they fanned us with huge peacock feathers fashioned into fans. They guided us down long corridors that had shiny smooth hardwood floors inlaid with mother-of-pearl and precious stones. I felt tempted to remove my shoes and slide down the long corridors. Of course, I couldn't, but it would have been fun.

A servant girl guided us into a room where brilliant chandeliers hung from the ceiling, silk tapestries and beautiful pictures adorned the walls, and colorful Tibetan carpets lay on the floor. Golden candlesticks and other fragile, lavish ornaments decorated the room. I stood still, hesitant to move, afraid I might break something. Then I remembered my mother's advice to take five deep breaths, and as I did I relaxed a little.

The servant invited us to sit and have a refreshing mango *lassi* to drink with a little snack of *chatamari*.

"Since you've never been in the presence of the monarch," the servant said, "I will teach you what to do when you meet the royal King Birendra . . . "

"First, remove your shoes . . . " *I guess we didn't need to buy new shoes after all.*

"Enter the room bowing low before the king. Be very humble. Don't speak until he speaks to you."

"Always address the king as *His Holy Majesty, King of the Lands of the Nepalese People and Knight of the Holy.*"

"Don't use the word *you* but instead say *mausuf* which means 'Your majesty,' and don't ask his majesty any questions unless he offers you the opportunity. Only respond to what he says to you."

Finally she concluded, "When you depart, bow again very low and back out of the room. Never show your back to the king."

Then she informed us, "We will meet back in this room after your audience with the king."

I felt so nervous, I wished I could run away or hide, but at the same time I was intrigued by all the unusual things I was learning and seeing.

The king must have made a mistake, he must have meant to summon someone else. Why would the king want to see me a poor, little, peasant boy? What do I have or know that the king wants? I didn't bring the king any special gifts.

My thoughts were interrupted by a knock on the door. Another servant appeared and announced: "The king is ready to see Mr. Sonam Sherpa and Mr. Mingma Sherpa."

Phura Tharkey explained, "We will follow the servant who will lead us to the king."

The servant led us down another corridor that led to the throne room. As we walked, I almost tripped over my own feet, I was so nervous.

We arrived at a beautiful doorway that had intricate carvings on it. The servant told us, "This door opens into the throne room where the king will have an audience with you."

We removed our shoes, then the servant opened the door and led us into the most beautiful room in the whole palace! There was a stunning, long red carpet that led to an ornate throne. I worried I might trip on the carpet, but the servant bowed low and walked at a slow pace. Uncle and I focused on the servant and followed him. I was startled when I discovered we were at the end of the long, red carpet.

We stayed bowed until the king spoke. "It is a pleasure to meet you, Mr. Sonam Sherpa and Mr. Mingma Sherpa. Thank you, Phura Tharkey, you have done well to bring them to me."

Phura Tharkey looked so pleased to hear those words from the king. He had feared that he had fallen out of favor with the king since our arrival in Kathmandu had been delayed.

Slowly we lifted our heads, looked up, and saw King Birendra *with his crown upon his head* as I had hoped. He was seated on a dazzling, golden throne smiling down at us.

When I saw his smile, his crown and his throne, joy bubbled up inside of me! We had been so afraid we would make a mistake, but the king's smile made us feel welcome.

King Birendra spoke to us. "Please be seated. My servant will bring tea for all of us."

As we waited for the tea, the king asked "How was your trip to Kathmandu?"

Uncle replied: *"His Holy Majesty, King of the Lands of the Nepalese People and Knight of the Holy,* the walk was good, but the airplane ride was scary. I am glad we made it here without any problems."

The king asked, "What was your favorite part of the trip, Sonam?"

I spoke his long title, as Uncle had before, responding, "There were many new things to see, and I was thankful that we stopped at several places so I could draw pictures of them. I have special paper that an Austrian climber gave me, and each day during our trip to Kathmandu I drew pictures on it."

"I would like to see your drawings," the king replied, "but first, there's one thing I'd like you to do for me. I want you to draw a picture of the elephant in the courtyard. I love elephants! I love them so much that I had twenty-three elephants at my coronation."

"His Holy Majesty, King of the Lands of the Nepalese People and Knight of the Holy, it is my honor and pleasure to make your wish come true. The elephant is a regal and grand animal. We saw your elephant, Prem Prasad, when we arrived at the palace grounds, and yesterday we saw where your coronation took place. It is a fascinating, beautiful place."

The king's voice was pleased, "Oh, you know my elephant's name! This is wonderful! After tea, you will go with my servant out to the courtyard and when you have finished drawing Prem Prasad, I would like you to bring his picture to me."

After we receded from the room backward as the servant had taught us, I turned to Uncle. "Did the king summon me all the way to Kathmandu only to draw a picture of his elephant? That seems absurd to me."

"I don't know, maybe he has another reason that he hasn't revealed yet," Uncle speculated.

I felt fortunate to have a special bond with the king: we both loved and revered elephants! As I drew the elephant for King Birendra, I thought of Ganesh, the elephant god.

Ganesh has treated me well. He has blessed me with artistic skills; he helped me get my copper box lid back from the monkey; and now Ganesh has created this special bond between me and the king.

I decided I would draw two different pictures of the elephant to play a little trick on the king. Along with the king's elephant, I'd incorporate a tiny, almost invisible picture of Lord Ganesh into one of the drawings.

Would the king even notice Ganesh? I wondered.

I planned to draw a second picture of Prem Prasad without Ganesh in it, just in case the King didn't like Ganesh in the picture.

In each picture, the elephant will be in a different position, I decided.

When I had finished both drawings, the servant escorted us back into the palace to present the pictures to the king. Phura Tharkey, Uncle and I followed the servant, and again we bowed low as we walked slowly down the red carpet.

King Birendra greeted us and asked to see the picture I had drawn.

"*His Holy Majesty, King of the Lands of the Nepalese People and Knight of the Holy,* here is my humble attempt to draw your magnificent elephant. I hope you like it."

As the king looked at the drawings, a little smile crossed his face. "Ah, you are so clever, Sonam! You have included Ganesh in your drawing! This is spectacular. You will go far in your life, and I will put this drawing in my private quarters so I can look at it daily."

Then more formally King Birendra stated, "Now, since we have only a few more minutes for our time together, I imagine you would like to know why I summoned you."

I nodded, my whole body attentive and ready to hear what the king would say.

"I have a problem that I know you, Sonam Sherpa, can solve for me."

I was excited. *Now at last, I will get the answer to all the things I have wondered about!*

"I feel a need to *see* the people who live in my kingdom. I also need *them* to know that I care for them so they understand that I make laws to benefit them all. But because my many kingly duties in Kathmandu occupy my time, I cannot go myself to the places where all my people live. I need you, Sonam, along with my emissary Phura Tharkey, to go throughout my kingdom to represent me."

Then he gave his decree, "You will go to many different parts of my kingdom, greet the people there for me, and draw pictures of them, their villages, and the landscape, so that when you bring these pictures back to me, I will be able to see my people and our country. The reason I have chosen you, Sonam, to do this project with Phura Tharkey is because you are such a fine artist! I prefer your drawings to a photograph because your drawings show so well how people feel."

I was shocked. *This doesn't make sense! I'm sure the king has never even seen any of my drawings.* It was hard to believe what the king was asking me to do.

I also thought, *It's a great honor to be chosen by the king to do this special project, but if I go all around the kingdom to draw pictures, I'll never be able to go to school! And who will take care of my parents in their old age? And guard my sheep?*

Then as if reading my mind, the king reached over and picked up a large envelope from to the table beside his throne. Opening it, he withdrew a few pieces of paper which he handed to us. I was astonished!

I recognized the pictures as soon as I saw them. *These are the drawings of my village that I gave to the Austrian climber!*

"You see Sonam, I do have some of the pictures that you have drawn," he said with glee in his eyes. "You are talented, your drawings are superb and beautiful! You capture the essence of the hard lives my people live, the activities of village life, the grandeur of the beautiful mountain scenery as well as the tiniest, exquisite details of plant and animal life!"

My eyes widened and my mouth fell open in total surprise! Thoughts raced through my mind. *How did the king get these pictures? I've never been to Kathmandu before. I've never met the king or anyone from the palace.*

Then I remembered the day Hans, the Austrian climber, had visited our village. Hans had given me some drawing paper and pastels and in exchange, I had drawn some pictures and given them to him.

But didn't Hans say he planned to take them home to his eleven-year-old son?

As Phura Tharkey studied the pictures, a smile crossed his face. "I am so glad to have the opportunity to view these fine drawings, the ones you told me about in Khumjung. I thought I'd never get to see them."

The king continued with his story. "A few days ago, I hosted an audience of some foreign dignitaries. Each is Secretary of Natural Resources in his own country. Every country represented at this meeting has spectacular natural beauty and resources that we all want to manage to the best of our abilities. We met to discuss the successes and challenges we face in our own countries. I told the dignitaries that it makes me sad that I rarely have the opportunity to go to the mountains and the Terai to meet with the people who live in my kingdom. One of the visiting dignitaries, a man from Austria, offered to show me some pictures of villagers and life in the mountains. He said they had been drawn by a very talented, delightful boy named Sonam Sherpa."

When he said that, I got goosebumps all over. *This is unbelievable!*

In his deep voice, the king continued, "I was so enthralled by the beautiful pictures that I had a deep desire to meet the young artist, you Sonam Sherpa, and for that reason I summoned you to the palace."

Wow! This is the answer to all the questions I've asked myself throughout this journey. This is the reason the king summoned me to the palace. I never in a thousand years would have guessed!

"Sonam, I have seen a lot of art, and a Newari artist lives in the palace. He paints pictures of the palace, the life of the royalty, and religious *tankas*, but your style is unique. The pictures you drew are so fine that in addition to the project I put before you and Phura Tharkey, I want to hang some of them in the palace. I also want to include others in a traveling, international, children's art exhibit that Hans, the Austrian climber told me about."

I was so surprised my mouth dropped open, but no words of gratitude came out.

Uncle Mingma saved me. "His Holy Majesty, King of the Lands of the Nepalese People and Knight of the Holy, this is quite an honor. Our family and village folk will be astonished and pleased to know how much you value our young boy's drawings! We are all grateful for your recognition of his talent. Thuche, Dhanyabad."

"Sonam, it is always a good idea to reciprocate." The king asked me, "Do you understand what that means? You will do this for me, and now I ask, is there anything you would like me to do for you?"

I was scared to ask but then I remembered what my father had told me, "Nothing risked, nothing gained."

Stuttering a bit, I asked, "H-H-*His Holy Majesty, King of the Lands of the Nepalese People and Knight of the Holy,* I . . . I . . . I do have one question. Have you heard of a school called Budhanilkantha?"

The king's eyes lit up and his eyebrows lifted with curiosity, "Sonam, tell me how you know about this school."

I felt shy, but I told the King my whole story concluding, "I want to go to an excellent secondary school. My parents want me to become well educated, but they don't have enough money to pay for school. It might be possible for me to assist my uncle when he builds houses, but he doesn't have much money to pay me. There is a secondary school in Lukla that we tried to visit when we passed through, but it was closed due to earthquake damage. When we met the headmaster, he told us it is full for the next two years. My teacher in Khumjung told me about Budhanilkantha school, and she said it is an excellent school, but the entrance exam was scheduled to occur on the day after we left Khumjung. I am the top student in my school, and I won the art contest, but due to these obstacles, my chances of continuing my education are almost zero. I may have to be content to be a shepherd, but my life's dream is to go on to secondary school at the excellent Budhanilkantha School."

"Yes, I know this school well," King Birendra replied. "My family founded it, my own children attend the school, and the headmaster is my good friend. I am aware that you are a very serious and smart student, as well as a talented artist. The Budhanilkantha School would be an excellent place for you to study. I will talk with the headmaster tomorrow and ask him to give you the entrance exam while you are here in Kathmandu. After you pass it, we will arrange for you to have a scholarship. You can study at the school, and on the school vacations you and Phura Tharkey will go out to the villages where you will draw pictures of village life for me."

I was so excited I could have jumped out of my skin! I could not believe that my wildest dream was coming true!

I wanted to scream for joy, but instead, in a quiet, sincere voice full of gratitude, I spoke, *"His Holy Majesty, King of the Lands of the Nepalese People and Knight of the Holy*, I am honored and excited to be given these gifts. Thuche, Dhanyabad. My father will also be elated because he wants me to have an excellent education."

Uncle Mingma agreed, *"His Holy Majesty, King of the Lands of the Nepalese People and Knight of the Holy*, our whole family and village are very honored and pleased to receive this extraordinary gift."

The king looked pleased. "Sonam, with your skills and determination, your willingness to take a risk and ask for what you want, it's clear to me that you will indeed go far in life. It is my pleasure to support you along your way."

Glossary and Map

Buddhist/Buddhism

a person who practices Buddhism—a widespread Asian religion or philosophy. Buddhism was founded in northeastern India in the 5th century BC by Siddartha Gautama, who became known as "the Buddha." Tibetan Buddhism emphasizes compassion and selflessness in order to reach enlightenment. It is a pacifist religion focused on the preservation and respect for living things and liberating people and animals from suffering. (See Nirvana below.)

Celsius

a temperature scale. One degree Fahrenheit is 5/9 of a degree Celsisus. For example: 35 degrees Celsius = 95 degrees Fahrenheit.

Chai

a type of tea made by boiling tea leaves with milk, sugar, and cardamom.

Chapati

a round, flat, unleavened bread of India that is usually made of whole wheat flour and cooked on a griddle.

Chatamari

a little pizza.

Chorten

a Tibetan stupa.

Dal bhat

lentil (dal) curry soup served with steamed rice (bhat) and various side dishes such as steamed vegetables, pickle, poppadoms (flat crispy tortillas made of chickpea flour).

Dhanyabad

thank you in Nepali language.

Himal

the northern region of Nepal where the extremely high Himalaya mountains are located.

Himalayan Tahr

a heavy, goat-like black animal, with horns and a massive amount of fur, especially around its neck. It is (in 2023) on an international list of animals that are at high risk of global extinction.

Hindu/Hinduism

a person who practices Hinduism, a major religion and cultural tradition of South Asia. Hindu people worship many natural forces. Multiple gods and goddesses (Vishnu, Brahma, Shiva) are forms of these forces. The Hindu holy texts are called the Vedas and are written in early Sanskrit.

Hajur

in Nepali language, a term of respect that means "sir."

Kathmandu

the capital city of Nepal.

Khata

Tibetan ceremonial scarf traditionally made of silk. It is usually white symbolizing the pure heart of the giver.

Koi

a variety of carp fish that are kept for decorative purposes in outdoor ponds or water gardens. Koi can be white, black, red, orange, yellow, blue, brown or cream colored.

Kukri

a long, thick-bladed, curved knife.

Lama

a spiritual leader or teacher of Tibetan Buddhism.

Lassi

a smoothie-like beverage made of yogurt, water, spices (cumin and cardamom) and either fruit or salt.

Mandala

a geometric configuration of symbols made in the form of a circle, often made of colored sands. A mandala is a symbolic picture of the universe. It represents an imaginary palace that is contemplated during meditation.

Mani walls

stone walls carved with the six-syllable mantra, "Om mani padme hum," a form of prayer in Tibetan Buddhism. The English translation is "the jewel in the lotus."

Mantra

words or sounds to aid in meditation.

Mausuf

Your majesty, or royal king, in Nepali language.

Meter

1 meter = about 3.3 feet. The altitude of Kathmandu is 1400 meters = 4,300 feet. Khumjung is 3790 meters = 12,400. Mount Everest is 8,848.86 meters = 29,032 feet.

Namaste (NA-ma-stay)

a greeting showing respect. It generally means "The light in me honors the light in you."

Newar

an ethnic group of people, the indigenous inhabitants of the Kathmandu Valley and its surrounding areas. Newars are known for their contributions to culture, art, literature, trade, agriculture and cuisine. Their religions are Hinduism and Buddhism.

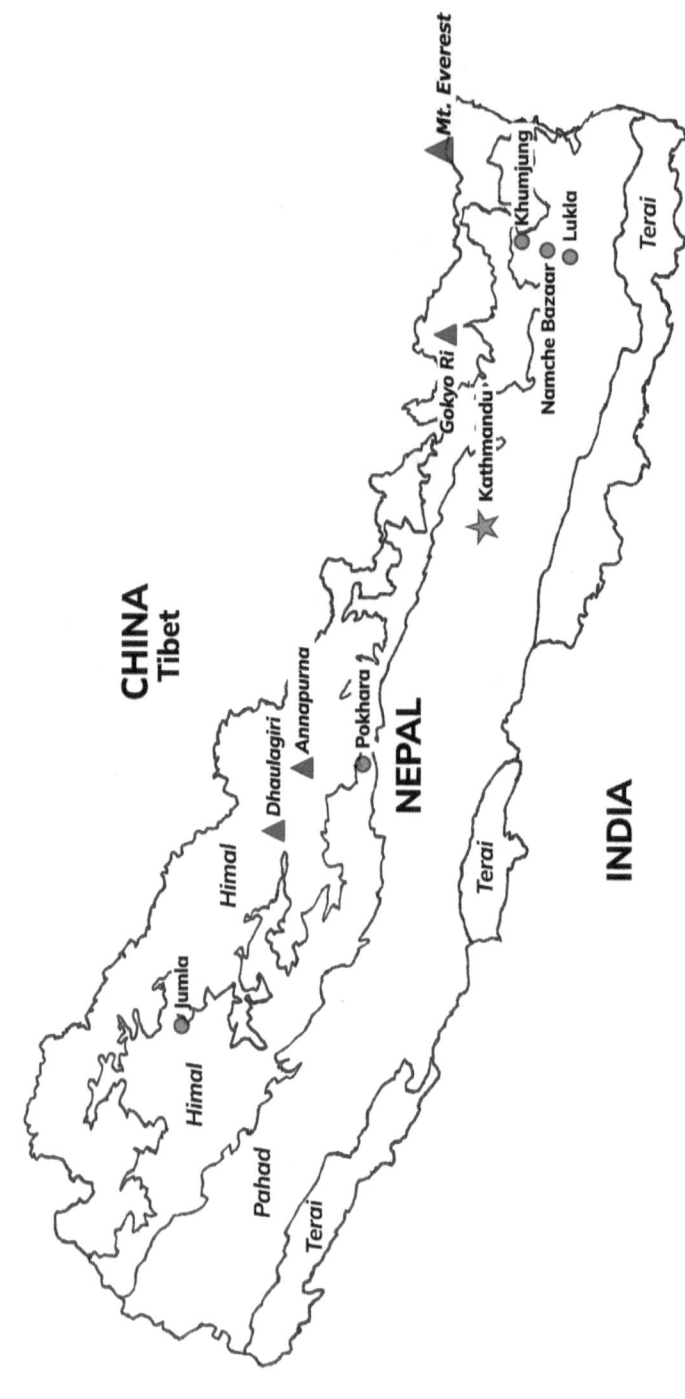

Mount Everest
  Sonam's papa guides climbers up this mountain, the world's highest

Khumjung
  Sonam's home village

Namche Bazaar
  Saturday market

Lukla
  world's most dangerous airport, built by Sherpas and Hillary

Gokyo Ri
  author trekked here from Lukla (see Author's Note)

Kathmandu
  capital of Nepal, King's palace

Terai
  kidnapper and vendor were from Terai (See Glossary)

Mustang
  ancient cave paintings were found here

Dhaulagiri
  Watters lived and worked close to here (see Author's Note)

Jumla
  guide Tej Bikram Shahi lives here in western Nepal (see Author's Note)

Himal
  high mountains, Himalayas (See glossary)

Pahad
  hilly region (See glossary)

137

Nepal

a small country north of India and south of China with three ecological zones: lowlands, mid-hills, and high mountains. Nepal is home of the world's highest mountain, Sagarmatha, also known as Mount Everest.

Nirvana

the ultimate spiritual goal in Buddhism. Reached when all want and suffering are gone. Believed to be the end of the cycle of death and rebirth. To reach it one must follow the 8-fold path—meditate regularly, have the right view, right intention, right speech, right action, right livelihood, right effort, and right mindfulness.

Partetu

potato patch.

Rickshaw

a hooded, passenger cart for 1-2 people, pulled by a person riding a cycle. It has three wheels—two under the passenger seat and one under the cyclist.

Prayer wheels

Prayer wheels come in various sizes ranging from giant to hand-held ones. They are made of metal, wood, stone, leather, or coarse cotton. On the outside of the wheel is written a mantra. Inside the wheel is a roll of paper upon which prayers are written. It is believed that every time someone turns the prayer wheel the person gains merit as the prayer circles the person's heart. Some prayer wheels are placed in temples and others in nature, where they are turned by the wind or river water.

Sadhu

a holy man, sage, or ascetic.

Saffron incense
incense used to alleviate anxiety, fever, headache and cough; often used before a person leaves on a long journey.

Sarangi
a wooden, 4-string, violin-like instrument.

Sel roti
fried sweet bread, similar to a donut.

Sherpa
an ethnic group of people who originated in Tibet and migrated in the 1200s to the high mountains in Nepal. They are known for their excellent climbing and trekking skills. Many Sherpas are porters and guides but not all porters and guides are Sherpa.

Stupa
a dome-shaped Buddhist shrine used to house relics of the Lord Buddha.

Tankas
brightly colored paintings depicting the life of Buddha or religious deities.

Tarkari
vegetable curry.

Terai
the lowland, grassy region in southern Nepal; a tropical, moist zone of deciduous vegetation with hot, humid summers and dry winters. Exotic animals including elephants, rhinos, and tigers live in the steamy jungle.

Tibetan tea
a tea made of yak butter, salt, tea leaves, a little wheat flour and some small pieces of dried cheese.

Tika

a red dot of vermilion paste applied on the forehead, between the eyebrows. This spot is considered the center of wisdom and concentration. It is also the spot where the third, or spiritual, eye is said to reside.

Tongkok

a heavy black wool Sherpa dress with a long sleeve blouse and brightly colored, woven, striped apron.

Topi hat

a man's fabric hat that is flat when not being worn. It is a symbol of national unity.

Thuche

thank you, in Sherpa language.

Tihar

5-day Festival of Lights.

Yak

a large domesticated wild ox with shaggy hair, humped shoulders, and large horns; used for its milk, meat, hide and wool. It is used as a pack animal at high elevations.

Yeti

a large, possibly imaginary, hairy creature resembling a human or bear, said to live in the highest part of the Himalayas.

Author's Note

Nepal is a small country, in Asia, on the opposite side of the world from the USA.

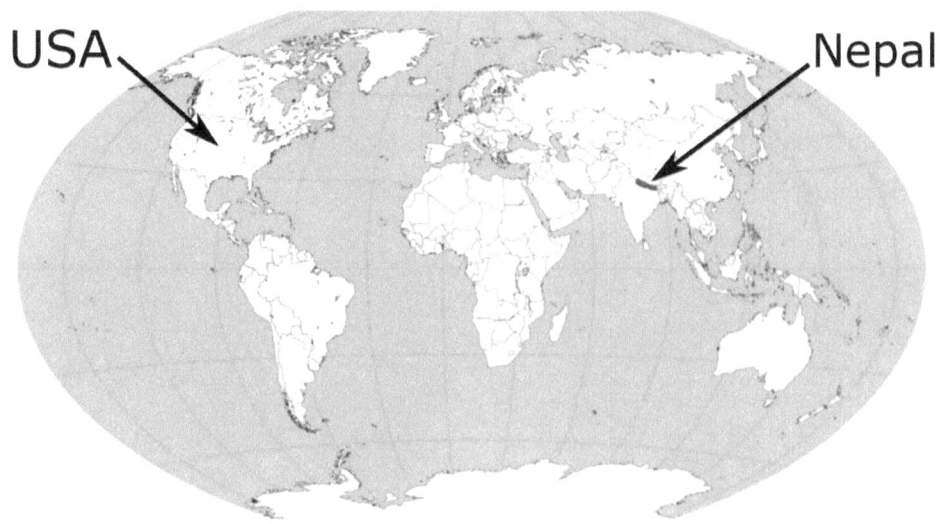

USA Nepal

In Nepal is a range of extremely high mountains called the the Himalayas. One of them, Mount Everest (whose Nepali name is Sagarmatha) is the world's highest mountain. The 29,032 foot (8,848.86 meter) peak was first summited by Sir Edmund Hillary and Sherpa Tenzing Norgay in 1953. Since then more than 6000 people have summited it.

Near Mount Everest is a village called Khumjung, the home of an ethnic group of people called Sherpa. Sherpas originated in Tibet then migrated to Nepal about 600 years ago. Many Sherpas are guides or porters for treks up Mount Everest.

Sonam's Surprise is set in Nepal in the 1970s. Although the story is fictional, I've stayed accurate to the facts about Nepal. It was inspired by a boy named Sonam whom I met there in the 1970s. Below is a photo of me with Sonam, standing near his school. Khumjung had both primary and secondary schools, but it was rare for villages to have both. Most students had to leave their villages to go to secondary school.

Tshiring Jangbu Sherpa

I met Sonam when my parents and I trekked to the Everest Base Camp in 1974.

How was *Sonam's Surprise* created?
The story behind the story

It takes a village to create a book.

The story started in 1974 in Nepal, when I wrote a short story about a boy named Sonam. I envisioned writing a group of short stories about kids from various countries who each entered a drawing in a traveling international art show. The only one I wrote was the Nepal story. I shared it with some children, but then it sat dormant in my attic for many years.

During that time, my connection to Nepal stayed alive through friends David and Nancy Watters*, and later their son Daniel. They worked in rural Nepal for numerous years. Their story can be found in the book *At the Foot of the Snows: A journey of faith and words among the Kahm speaking people of*

Nepal, by David E. Watters and sons. The family eventually returned to the USA, to Port Angeles, Washington, a city close to Seattle where I lived.

The story wanted to come out of hibernation and grow and be named. So, I took it out of my attic, dusted it off, and went to the Watters' home. I was given the privilege of writing at David's desk, inspired by large, beautiful photos of Nepal and books in Nepalese that surrounded me.

Many people helped *Sonam's Surprise* grow. You can find a comment or review of *Sonam's Surprise* by those with an asterisk (*) on our website.

Joyce Major, author of *The Orangutan Rescue Gang*, and Rita Golden Gelman, author of more than 70 children's books, guided me in the writing process. Rita also encouraged me to return to Khumjung, which I did in 2022.

Madeline Kellett*, a Canadian middle-grade literacy teacher whom I met in Cambodia on my way to Nepal, gave me some guidance and wrote an excellent review of *Sonam's Surprise*.

Mingma Sherpa*, a nanny for a woman I met in Seattle, answered many cultural questions. I was surprised and excited to learn that she grew up in the village next to Khumjung and that her father, Rita Lakpa Sherpa, was a guide for treks up Mount Everest, which he summited 17 times.

Tej Bikram Shahi*, a Nepali school headmaster and Nepal Travel Guide, was my trekking guide in 2022 for a two-week trek to Gokyo Ri, near Mount Everest. Under his guidance I returned to Khumjung. Tej loved the fictious character Sonam and often imagined things Sonam could be doing. He made the character come alive.

Niroj Bade, an artist whom I hired in Kathmandu in December 2022, became the illustrator.

I returned from my trip to Nepal in 2022, inspired to write, and *Sonam's Surprise* doubled in size to its present length.

Several people read the story and gave me valuable feedback:

Children: Charlotte, Cooper, and Mia.

Adults: Maria Stobie, Marilyn Love, Mary Edwards, Sasha Elias, Susan Howlett, and Suzanne Tedesko, all from Seattle. Alexander Kokic Schmidt from Australia, Daniel Watters, an American who lived 50 years in Nepal, and Tshiring Jangbu Sherpa*, all of whom I met in Nepal.

My professional staff: editors Sally Apokedak*, literary agent and teacher, and Cori Adler*, copy editor, Claudie C. Bergeron, cover artist, and Tom Sharp, publisher.

I am filled with deep appreciation and gratitude for all the help I was given. To honor those who helped, a portion of the profits from the sales of *Sonam's Surprise* will be donated to schools in Nepal. To learn about donations, go to https://sharpgiving.com/Nichols/SonamsSurprise.

About the author and illustrator

Nikki Nichols, author

Sonam's Surprise is Nikki Nichols' debut novel. It reflects her interests in cultural experiences, adventure, travel (70 countries total) and singing. In addition to these things, she enjoys photography, gardening, rowing crew, and volunteering. Nikki grew up in the San Francisco Bay area (3rd generation from Berkeley, California), but has lived most of her adult life in Seattle, Washington.

To contact Nikki, go to our website:
https://sharpgiving.com/Nichols/SonamsSurprise

Niroj Bade, illustrator

Niroj Bade is from the ancient, historical community, Bhaktapur, near Kathmandu, Nepal. He completed his Master of Fine Arts at Tribhuvan University in Kathmandu. He is fascinated by traditional cultures, festivals, and dances and enjoys painting pictures of them as well as of architecture and nature. He paints mostly with oil and acrylic paints, but he drew the pictures for *Sonam's Surprise* with pen and ink. To view more of his art, go to https://www.nirojbade.com.

When Niroj agreed to be the illustrator, he commented that he identified with Sonam because, when he was a young boy, he too liked to draw on the dirt and everywhere.

Book Club Questions

1. Who are the main **characters** in the story and what task was given to each? (see answers)

   What character would you like to be? Why?

2. Describe Sonam's **personality**. (see answers)

   At the beginning of the story, Sonam introduces himself as a curious person, yet when the king's messenger summons him, Sonam is not sure he wants to go? Why?

   What personality strengths does Sonam have that help him along his journey?

   As the story progresses, what changes do you see in Sonam?

3. Sonam wants something that will change his life, what is it? What are three things he did to obtain his **goal**? (see answers)

   What is something that you want for yourself that would take effort to obtain? What can you do to obtain that?

4. What did Sonam **carry** in his pocket? Why? (see answers)

   How could you protect yourself if you had to?

5. **Nature** has an impact on people's choices, opportunities, and well-being. What are some naturally occurring events that make it difficult to live in Nepal? (see answers)

   After the storm, the river flowed swiftly. Sonam's shoe came off and floated downstream.

   What would you do if you lost something of value that was hard to replace at the time you needed it?

6. **Art** is an important expression of the culture of a country. The king values art. How does Sonam's art contribute to his country? What are three things that students made for the school art show? (see answers)

What would you make?

7. What did Sonam and Apa do to try to help their **community**? (see answers)

What could you do to help your community?

Answers

1. **Characters:**

   Sonam—respond to the king's summons, draw pictures for his mother, and figure out how to get to secondary school

   Phura Tharkey—the king's messenger, lead Sonam and Uncle Mingma to the King

   Uncle Mingma—escort Sonam to the king, build stone houses

2. **Personality:** curious, excited, playful, helpful, creative (art & ideas), sneaky, smart, goal-oriented

3. **Goal:** To go to secondary school; figures out ways he could obtain money to pay for school; visits the school in Lukla; asks the king about the *Budhanilkantha* School

4. **Carry:** Two stones to fight off wolves or other problems

5. **Nature:** landslides, earthquakes, avalanches, storms

6. **Art:** carpet, statues, baskets, drawings

7. **Community:** pull out the survey stakes to deter foreigners from building a large hotel in a spot beloved by the village

For more questions and answers, go to our website:
https://sharpgiving.com/Nichols/SonamsSurprise